Purrfectly Kissed

A MAVERICK PRIDE TALE

THE MAVERICK PRIDE TALES

C.D. GORRI

Purrfectly Kissed:
A Maverick Pride Tale #2
by C.D. Gorri
Edited by BookNookNuts

Copyright 2020, 2022 C.D. Gorri, NJ

To my readers,
Never forget you are purrfect in every way!
Xoxo.
Del mare alla stella,
C.D.

Blurb

She's a curvy She-Cat searching for the purrfect kiss. He's a Black Bear who doesn't want a mate.

The Beta of the Maverick Pride has no desire to find a mate. He's tried that once, and all it got him was hurt. This grumpy Bear is content to be alone. Or is he?

Jessica Maverick has been searching for her fated mate since she was just a cub. But finding love is hard for the sister of the Pride Neta. How's a girl supposed to have a sex life with her big brother breathing down her neck?

Determined to find her mate, she seeks out Uncle Uzzi's impeccable advice.

Will this dauntless She-Cat catch her reclusive Bear?

Uzzi Stregovich was looking forward to his upcoming trip to Maverick Point, New Jersey with glee. The Tiger Pride Neta had settled down with the female Uzzi had rescued from a disastrous date, and now he wanted his service for the entire Pride.

His magic buzzed and hummed, that special gift from his ancestors alerting him that love was, in fact, in the air.

Uzzi was an old Witch. A descendant of the Goddess of Love, his powers were uniquely attuned to finding fated mates and pairing up supernaturals who would, undoubtedly, be better off together.

It was a gift and a responsibility he worked hard to maintain. Feeling the presence of his dearly departed wife, Uzzi settled down for some much needed meditation before his short journey.

"It will be alright, libeling. I have a feeling this first match will hardly need any interference at all."

With that thought, he smiled and sat down on the ancient carpet he used when trying to focus his powers.

Yes, this one will be bearish good fun.

Prologue

Uncle Uzzi stared at his calendar and shook his fuzzy white head. Could it really be this late in the season?

"Well, liebling, you were right. I need a new calendar system," he mused aloud.

His beloved wife, Betty, would have been tickled pink at his admission. The old Witch grunted a thanks as Richard, his housekeeper, sat a plate of just frosted black and white cookies and black tea on the table.

"Can I get you anything else?"

"No, thank you, Richard," he said, nodding at the man.

"In fact, I must call the car service. It looks like I

have a reservation with Maverick pride, and I must not be late."

"Yes, sir. I can wrap the leftovers for you to take," the older man added.

"Ah, yes. That would be lovely, thank you."

Uncle Uzzi approved of Richard's baking skills and was glad his wife had hired the man to come work for them once she'd entered hospice. His heart squeezed at the memories of her that came surging back into his brain whenever he thought of his liebling.

"I know, I know," he mumbled.

He felt the warm caress of her brush against his heart, and Uzzi stilled. Every now and then, he felt her energy as familiar and precious as his own.

She had been his true and fated mate in life and would remain part of his soul until they embarked on their next adventure, be it in this world or another. That was the thing about fated mates. Their souls belonged to one another.

Uzzi had already had his time on earth with his liebling, and as promised, he would dedicate the rest of his time to helping others find their soul mates.

"Come, I must get ready for my travels," he said to no one in particular.

"Get ready, Maverick Point. Uncle Uzzi's Magical

Matchmaking Service is coming to town, and you pussies are in for it now!"

His laughter rang out, followed by a spark of blue magic that was both warm and bright. There was nothing quite like news of a fated mate to deliver.

"And here we go."

Chapter One

S wirls of clouds, stark white against an azure sky circled the top of Mount Maverick, looming in the distance like some far away fairytale mountaintop.

Jessica pushed herself harder, racing across the frost covered forest on her four furry legs. She cut a path through the trees, reveling in the glory of a perfect winter's day.

The holidays were always hardest on her. Ever since both her parents had passed on, Jess had felt alone. True, she had a brother. Hunter Maverick had proved time and again that he was the best brother in the world. He'd been there through her somewhat difficult formative years. And yet, the man had never mistreated her over any of her teenaged tantrums and histrionics.

She was sure his Neta tendencies had often warred with his older sibling sympathy. Either way, the Alpha male had definitely gotten the short end of the stick when he'd had to take on the role of parent and Pride leader immediately after he'd finished college.

Jessica wasn't bad per se, but she had a fanciful imagination. Her inner beast chuffed and growled at the memories of her heart laden journals and tear stained pillows.

Grrrrrrr.

Truth was, she'd been dreaming of love everlasting and her mating ceremony, the equivalent of a wedding for normals, since before she'd even grown boobs. Once she'd received said knockers, she was all *look out Pride males*!

Poor Hunter hadn't known what to do when his green as grass sister had started sneaking around the Pride House, itching to catch a peak of his guards unclothed or mid-shift. That period of time had resulted in many a time out for the young female.

Sigh.

Well, how else was she supposed to learn about boys? Besides, Shifters were uninhibited when it came to nudity. Still, there was such a thing as etiquette.

Once Hunter had caught her staring in a rather un-Shifter-like way, he'd ordered all the men to change forms behind the house. Hell. He'd even had them construct a dressing room of sorts so they wouldn't walk around his baby sis nude.

The pussy-blocking jerk.

Double sigh.

It had been years since she'd thought of those troublesome times when puberty had clashed with common sense. Oh yeah, but Jessica never did anything half-assed.

If she was going to make a fool of herself, she was going all out. She had even fancied herself in love a time or two, *or maybe seven.* But each one of her would-be suitors, fuzzy-faced youths of course, had been run off by the big tough Neta. He always was a spoilsport.

High school had been one long running test of *how frustrated could a girl get before she kills her brother.*

Not that college was any better. But that was her fault for commuting. She should have known better than to take a brand new automobile as a bribe to live home and drive to all her classes.

Another weary sigh.

Her hymen was getting way too fucking comfortable inside of her. The damn thing thought it had tenure or something. One thing was certain, being an almost virgin sucked.

One time so did not count.

Especially *that* first time. Jessica was all about reclaiming her virginity these days. Might as well, since she could hardly call what happened between her and the lanky normal sex.

Ugh.

Her Tiger could not agree more. The striped beastie was eager to find a male, claim him, and start pumping out kids.

Grrrrrrrr.

Not that Jessica was exactly ready for that, but the rest of it. Yeah. Why the fuck not? Dating was more difficult than ever since Hunter had found his own mate, truly ascending to his rightful position as Neta. He'd been cleaning up the Pride left and right, and they were all the better for it.

But Jess was still alone. And that sucked.

What was wrong with men these days? Didn't they like sex?

Thankfully, Hunter had stopped harassing her about her non-existent sex life. He was too busy with his own mate to police his baby sister's dates.

Jessica's beast chuffed when she thought of the new Nari of the Pride. Elissa Phoenix, soon-to-be Maverick, if Jess's idiot brother ever got the woman to the altar, was simply amazing. The tiny blonde was everything Jessica wanted in a sister, and she was so happy for them both.

The couple was already expecting the next generation of Pride royalty, but for some reason the woman still did not have a ring on her finger.

SMH. Dope.

The least her big bro could do was make an honest woman of her. Weddings were not a Shifter thing, but Elissa had lived as a normal for most of her life until she'd been claimed and experienced the Puspa, turning her into a Tiger Shifter as well.

So yeah, Hunter definitely needed to step up and marry the woman before Jessica's new niece or nephew made an appearance.

Really? Does it look like I am unhappy or something, Jess?

The Nari of the Pride, and Jessica's closest girlfriend, pushed the thought inside her mind's eye.

The younger Tiger chuffed, having forgotten she wasn't alone for a minute. Jess had been running so fast and far through the gray and white woods, she'd been lost in her own thoughts.

Communicating telepathically wasn't something she did very often, but it was a treasured characteristic of close Pride mates.

Since Elissa was new to the whole thing, it was quite the surprise she could communicate that way at all. Having received the gift of *the blossoming*, the legendary transformation known amongst the ancient Bengali Shifter Tribes as Puspa, after she'd been claimed by her mate, she was discovering new abilities all the time.

Jessica was in complete awe of the female. So rare, it was now a myth among Tiger Shifters, the *Puspa* only happened when a couple was intertwined by destiny and blessed by the Fates.

With it, the human partner received the gift of an animal spirit and the ability to shift into that animal. But that only happened if the gods or Fates allowed it, and only if the recipient was deemed worthy.

Elissa had obviously been chosen. Jess bumped her head gently against the other female. Her Tiger was small and beautiful, just like the woman. She was strong, though.

The Nari would never be weak. And Jessica both loved and admired her new sister. She was genuinely happy for her brother, too.

Lucky fucker.

Sorry, Lissa, I was just lost in thought. Besides, I am not wrong. You need a ring, and my dumb brother is gonna get a smack if he doesn't go shopping soon!

She felt Elissa's responding laughter and joined her in her mirth.

Yeah, well, don't you worry. He loves me and I love him. We just need to set a date.

Jessica chuffed as her Nari moved slowly through a deep pile of snow. She stretched her paws, loving the way the chilly wind sifted through her fur when Elissa yelped.

Tigers don't yelp.

Elissa corrected Jessica.

Are you two ladies okay?

A deep, rumbling voice entered both their heads.

Jessica turned around to see a huge Black Bear ambling towards them. His coat shone deep and dark, a warm chestnut brown on the top of his head that gave way to longer, shaggier fur of deeper browns and blacks along his back and rump. He looked perfect in the woods, majestic even with the sunlight filtering through the pines.

He was enormous with claws that were easily five-inches long and razor sharp. Jessica's heart stopped, but she shook it off. She was good at pretending she did not notice him.

But of course, he would be there. Brayden Smith, Black Bear Shifter, and Maverick Pride Beta was there to guard the Nari.

It's not like he'd shown up for Jessica. If only, she mused, careful to keep her secret longing hidden. Truth was, ever since the big smack down with their evil former Beta, Blake, she'd been thinking nonstop about the big Bear.

One second, she'd been shoved by Blake so hard her head had cracked against the granite countertop. The next second, Brayden had come barreling in, swatting the Tiger like he was an annoying gnat. He'd picked her up and ran his hands over her from head to toe, checking and cataloguing her injuries.

She could almost feel them now. His big hands skating over her body with a gentleness she hadn't expected from the enormous Bear.

Chapter Two

S ighing inwardly, Jessica remembered her link, and worked double time to shield her thoughts and emotions from both Elissa and Brayden.

She didn't need to make any more of an ass of herself. Hadn't she done that by always running after Lance, the youngest of her brother's guards?

But that was a whole other thing. Not the unrequited love everyone seemed to think she felt.

Why did you yelp?

Brayden asked.

Oh, no. I mean, we're fine. Uh, I just stepped on a stone back there.

Jessica replied, and if Tigers could blush, hers would be beet red.

The Bear nodded and turned around, completely ignoring Jessica. That was pretty much par for the course these last few weeks.

Ever since that scene in the kitchen, Brayden had acted like she pretty much did not exist. Not that she understood why. Like at all.

Oh well.

If he hated her so much, Jess just would not bother him. Okay, so she'd been a little annoying with all the questions when he'd first joined the Pride.

But could she help it if he was interesting? The man was a Black Bear in a Pride full of Tiger Shifters.

She was curious. Like cats often were. It was simply part of her Tiger's nature.

Nowadays, he had no time for foolish females. He was the Beta, second to only Hunter in power and dominance.

Jessica shivered just thinking about all that muscle and strength. He was so tall and wide, covered in thick ropes of muscle. A real mountain of a man. Big enough to make a thick girl like her feel tiny.

And wasn't that something?

She exhaled a puff of air in the cold woods, whipping her tail back and forth as they neared the Pride House. She should have been thinking about work, her boutique, anything else. But her thoughts were all about Brayden Smith, the sinfully gorgeous Black Bear Shifter who didn't even know she was alive.

Sad chuff.

After they shifted to their skin, separately, of course, she watched him through lowered lids. His brown hair was thick and wavy on the top of his head, much like his bear's.

He wore a close-cropped beard she was dying to get her hands on at all times. But what she loved most were his near black eyes. Sometimes, when his emotions were heightened, they glittered like obsidian glass.

But now, when he was fresh from his Change, the color was so rich and warm, like fresh roasted espresso beans. There was something sad about them, though. Like he always held himself at a distance.

Maybe it was because he was a Bear in a Pride full of pussies.

Snort.

Jessica sobered quickly. Most likely, his reserve was due to a particularly disturbing rumor she'd heard about him years ago.

Jessica's heart squeezed in sympathy, hurting for the big, beautiful man. She might dream about mates and true love's kiss, but he'd had all that. Much to her own dismay.

Brayden Smith had had a true mate, and he'd lost her. It was a tragic accident, as far as Jessica knew.

He'd been at work when the young Sow had went driving during a freak thunderstorm. Jessica didn't know the details, only that the woman had hit a slick in the road and had gone careening into a tree at full speed. She'd died upon impact.

That said, Jessica supposed it was only natural for him to be reticent around females. Not that there were many in the Maverick Pride.

As a whole, there were maybe fifty or sixty Pride mates, and out of that, maybe a dozen and a half were females. And again, only a little more than half of those were of age to find a mate.

Needless to say it had been lonely for Jessica growing up in Maverick Point. It was probably the reason Brayden liked the place.

No swarm of women following him around, throwing themselves at his spectacular *shoe size fifteen* feet. He'd even turned down Pamela Brown.

Lance had told her so. Pamela was a female Tiger in the Maverick Pride. The woman seemed hard and was always a little too stuck up to be friends with Jess. She thought she was a gift from the gods. The way she threw herself at all the men just because she was skinny and tall.

Hmmpf.

Jessica's she-Cat was not approving of the female. Even when they were children, Pamela was different. Mean and a little bullying. But she was part of the Pride, so Jess tolerated her. As the Neta's sister, it was her duty to be above the petty squabbles the other females engaged in.

Sometimes that really sucked. Like big time.

Especially when they were all pining to be just another notch in the bedposts of so many of the males. Especially her brother's guards.

Pierce, Lance, Reg, Mikey, and Brayden were all very sought after. Not to mention Hunter himself, who'd been on the *most wanted* list since he ascended to his position.

Luckily, Elissa had arrived just in time. Jessica still could not believe she used to chase Lance around like some love-struck cub.

Heat burned her cheeks at the memory. The Tiger had been kind, but firm in letting her know he didn't see her that way. She saw he was right immediately, and Jessica was more than fine with just being friends.

Really, she was. She was just lonely.

Oh well, she would not be throwing herself at him again. But Jessica still wanted a mate. There was just one problem, where was she going to find an eligible man?

She knew better than to moon over the big Bear Shifter. Even though his lips looked unbelievably soft and kissable. His body was definitely nibble-able.

Was that even a word?

Fuck it.

If it wasn't, she just invented it,

Nibbleable.

It definitely had potential. But even so. Jessica had to recognize the very sexy, very off limits, Brayden Smith was not for her.

Doubly sad chuff.

She waited while Elissa shifted back to human. It took a little extra. Her being pregnant and all.

The Nari's tail had weaved back and forth as they'd trekked over the frozen ground back to the changing room behind the Pride House.

Elissa's slightly swollen belly had wobbled from side to side in her Tiger's body and Jess grinned happily. It was positively adorable.

Oh, shush it! I am a grown ass woman and only my mate can call me adorable, Jess.

Elissa scolded her.

Jessica frowned. She'd been projecting again and this time in her skin.

Well, shit.

She turned her head from side to side, but there was no sign of the big Black Bear. Wherever he was, she just hoped it was far enough away to keep from reading her thoughts.

Elissa was the only one allowed to be present to witness her humiliatingly lustful thoughts for the Bear.

The last thing she wanted was for big, sexy Brayden Smith to know she daydreamed about kissing him, for fuck's sake.

Growl.

Moan.

Sigh.

Prrrrrrrrrrrrrrrr.

Chapter Three

Brayden walked as fast as he could away from the females without drawing attention to himself. He had no use for women, but he liked the Pride Nari, and it was his job to protect her.

Occasionally, when the Neta's duties could not be avoided, Brayden was assigned to keep the Nari safe. Especially since the female was still getting used to her animal.

Shifters needed to transform into their animals to keep the balance between their dual natures. This was an understanding all Shifters were born with, even ones as different as Bears and Tigers.

No one had experienced the ancient Tiger blessing of Puspa in years, and so, the Pride did not know what to expect from their Nari. Already, it was strange how the urge to shift was not as strong with her yet.

But Brayden knew that feeling would only increase once she birthed the Alpha pair's cub. To prepare for that time when her inner beast would push for the Change, Elissa had announced her intention to practice daily.

Typically, Hunter would be the one to accompany her, but the male had a meeting with city and state officials that morning concerning Maverick Development.

The construction company where most of the Pride worked, including Brayden, kept them solvent. Along with a rather impressive stock portfolio, the Pride had plenty of money.

But work was necessary to keep the area's Shifters honest and loyal. They craved challenges and physical outlets to release energy. Fighting and fucking were always there, but Brayden preferred work.

When Hunter could not be with his mate, he'd ordered Brayden, the new Beta, to take over guard duty. He rarely minded, as it was Reg who often joined him in guarding the Nari.

But not today. Reg was working a double shift on

the access road they'd been repaving. He'd thought the female would cancel, but not their Nari. She was tenacious.

Besides, she was not alone. Today, *she* was there to accompany Elissa.

Jessica Maverick was hell on Brayden's system.

Even in her fur, she was radiant. Every time he saw the woman, he damn near swallowed his tongue. His Bear rose inside him, possessive about the curvaceous beauty and it was all he could do to rein in the animal.

But damn. The redheaded beauty was a certifiable knockout. A dream of a woman, unfortunately, she was also the Neta's little sister. In other words, the she-Cat was completely off limits.

Mine, grunted his Bear.

A rumbling growl built inside him, and Brayden worked hard to shut that shit down.

And fast.

He had no use for that kind of thinking. He'd been mated once, or as near to it as he could get. Once upon a time when he'd been younger, honor bound, and stupid as fuck.

He'd made it his responsibility to care for a little Sow from his hometown of Barvale. The Bear Clan where he'd been raised was named after the town, and it was a really nice place to live.

About a forty-minute drive from Maverick Point, the Barvale Clan was small and mostly made up of Black Bear Shifters, with the odd Grizzly and Brown mixed in. Rumor had it a group of Polar Bears had joined them as a special security unit.

He hadn't met them yet, but he was sure he would, eventually. Barvale was too close for him not to run into them. Even though he'd tried his best to avoid his old Clan.

The Devlins were in charge, and they ran it well. It wasn't like they had mistreated him badly or anything like that. Far from it.

Marcus Devlin was the Alpha, and he was damn good at running Barvale. All of them were good, honest Bears. He just couldn't stay there.

Not after the accident.

Fuck.

He hated thinking about it, but no matter how hard he tried, it was always there. And so was the guilt.

It was his fault Valerie had died. The Sow had only mated him after his best friend, her *true mate*, had gone off to Iraq after his unit had been called.

Enlisting at a young age, the fool was headstrong

and bent on protecting his country. It should have been nothing, an easy tour. But he'd been killed in an explosion when sweeping for roadside bombs.

John Beverwyck had been more than his best friend. He'd been like a brother to Brayden. Losing him had broken something inside both Valerie and Brayden, and they'd turned to each other for comfort.

We were so fucking young.

His Bear groaned long and hard at the memories. Sex was always complicated, but this had damn near destroyed him.

After that one night together, Brayden had vowed to do right by Valerie. He'd asked her parents for her hand, and they hastily agreed. Especially when she'd shown signs of bearing.

He'd been so young and idealistic. Thought it would all work out, even though his Bear was full of sorrow and heartbroken over his lost brother.

Brayden should have suspected something terrible that day he'd left for work. Valerie had been depressed for weeks, but that morning she was bright and cheerful.

An echo of the young girl he'd known when John was alive and the two of them had been dating. He could almost smell her cherry blossom perfume and see the twinkle in her dark eyes as she said goodbye to him for the last time.

"I'll be back late. The manager planned a meeting at four-thirty. The next train after that isn't until seven," he'd told her.

Guilt still racked him at the relief he'd felt at coming home late. The less time he'd spent with Valerie, the calmer his Bear was.

The animal had acknowledged her pregnant state with a sniff, but even his beast had known something was off or wrong.

Not wanting to know what it was, Brayden ignored his instincts. Hoping things worked themselves out, instead of putting in the effort to fix them himself. It was a coward's way, and he was ashamed of how he'd acted.

Fuck.

I should have protected her. Gotten her help.

Later that afternoon, he'd been pulled from his meeting with earth shattering news. Valerie was dead and the infant she carried in her womb was gone with her.

Bear and man still carried the responsibility for both their deaths. The weight of them sat heavily on his broad shoulders.

That was why he would never take a mate. He

couldn't. Brayden was underserving and unworthy. He would remain unmated and alone.

Forever.

His animal snarled and roared in pain, but the beast would just have to get over it. Loneliness was the only sure thing in his future. The only thing he could bank on.

He had a Pride now, and that helped. But no matter how fucking cute his Bear thought Jessica Maverick was, the she-Cat was off limits.

Never happening.

Rooooooaaaaaaaar.

Chapter Four

Brayden shook his head as he ambled out of the forest. The females were safe, and it was better for everyone if he got the fuck out of there.

He made his way to the back of the Pride House. He entered his suite of rooms through his private balcony and jumped right in the shower.

The custom-built stall was enormous. Big enough for a Bear to move around in. It was cold as hell outside, and the steaming water felt good over his skin.

The original bathroom had been larger than any typical one, but at six-foot seven-inches tall and two-hundred and eighty pounds, he'd needed more space.

It was a good thing he was in the construction business.

Even the specially built facilities of the Pride House were a little bit tight for Brayden. Typically, Tiger Shifters had leaner builds than Bears, though the Neta was wider than the rest of them.

Brayden still towered over everyone in the Pride. Something that used to get his hackles up. He supposed it wasn't anyone's fault. Shifters were physical creatures and shows of dominance were the norm.

But it got old fast. Always wondering if some idiot would throw a challenge his way. Now that he was the Pride Beta, it was only a matter of time before some young Tiger thought he could take on the huge Black Bear Shifter.

Grrr.

Brayden hoped to discourage that by his consistent display of loyalty and strength within the Pride itself. He was now foreman of his own construction crew for Maverick Development, and they were a strong group of males, trustworthy too.

The work was hard but satisfying. Their government contracts meant the crew did a lot of highway work. Recently they'd been taking down old overpasses on the highway and replacing them with new, sturdier constructs.

There was an old joke about New Jersey being nice once they finished building it. Now he understood what they meant.

Fact was, the Garden State was busy as fuck. So much traffic went up and down the highways they were constantly in need of repair and renovation. But out of everywhere he'd travelled, Jersey still had the sleekest highways.

Maverick Development was top notch too. Hunter made sure all his crews used the most environmentally conscious methods and supplies to complete all construction work.

The fact that Shifters got the work done at twice the speed of normals just meant the company usually won the contracts. Brayden was damn good at his job.

He liked working with his hands. It provided an excellent outlet for the Bear. It was no fun squashing young cubs who thought he was getting too old to throw down.

Nah.

They were too easily defeated, cowering under his Bear's might. But tearing down walls and building bridges?

Fuck yeah.

That was much more his speed. He had no interest in fighting, even if Shifters were a blood-thirsty bunch. Sometimes, it was necessary to prove a point or to stop someone from getting seriously injured.

At those times, he had no issue showing his strength. Even now, his Black Bear rippled and rumbled inside him. Fucking animal wouldn't be so anxious to knock some heads together if he would just settle the fuck down already.

Mate, the Bear grumbled.

Brayden closed his eyes, pushing the beast back with a firm *no.*

His cell phone beeped as he tugged on a pair of jeans and black long-sleeved shirt.

Fuck.

Hunter was back and he'd brought a guest. Nerves tightened his belly. Brayden sat down hard on the bed and tugged on his socks before stuffing his large feet into a pair of black leather work boots.

Uzzi Stregovich, famous amongst supernaturals for *Uncle Uzzi's Magical Matchmaking Service* was at the Pride House.

And what's more, Brayden was to attend a meeting with the old white haired Witch, as were all the eligible members of the Pride, at the Neta's behest.

Brayden groaned and rubbed his temples. As Beta, he was granted the honor of seeing the old Witch first. When he'd tried to refuse, Hunter had put his foot down.

The Neta, in his own happiness, wanted everyone to be afforded the same opportunity. Because Uzzi had brought him his mate, Hunter was sure the old magical matchmaker could do the same for everyone in the Pride.

Brayden tried to refuse one more time, but Hunter was not hearing that. he'd told the Bear to get his furry ass in gear. And it was too late to run now. Not that he would. The Maverick Pride was his home.

Fuck.

Maybe he could skirt the honor of being the first new client to someone else? Brayden didn't need Uzzi Stregovich and his *hoo-doo-voo-doo-super-matchmaking-senses* fucking with his life.

He was destined to be alone.

Period.

End of story.

Then why can't you stop thinking about a certain sexy redhead, his Bear growled inside his mind's eye.

Fuck. Off.

He told his Bear. Fucking bastard looked downright smug as he sat chilling in the metaphysical plane where he rested till called.

Want mate, the animal insisted.

No. Never. Not happening.

Grrrrrrrrr.

Brayden rolled his shoulders, quieting his Bear with a firm command. He'd go see Uncle Uzzi because he was told to by his Neta.

Not for any other reason.

Brayden did not want a mate.

That's what you think.

Fucking stubborn ass Bear.

Brayden shook his head and walked to the main living room area, stopping in his tracks at the sight that greeted him.

Double fuck.

Jessica Maverick was bent over at the waist trying to tug a pair of leggings over her rounded hips and failing miserably.

Holy Shit.

Why wasn't she using the changing room round the back? He wondered and tried to stop his cock from hardening perceptively in his jeans as he stared at the woman's perfect heart-shaped ass in the barely-there pink panties she wore.

Her firm cheeks peeked out of the Brazilian cut bottoms, giving him an unhindered view of her supple flesh. How he wanted to nibble that pert little bottom of hers.

Grrrr.

No. Fuck.

He closed his eyes tight and moved. He was at mid-turn with the intention of giving her some privacy when she caught sight of him.

"Brayden! Oops, uh look I am so sorry. And please don't tell my brother I was getting dressed in here, but the door to the changing room outside is frozen shut, and I didn't want to track mud all the way to the guest room," she explained.

She wiggled her ass, getting the tights over her gorgeous curves, then pulled an oversized sweater over her head. The flash of dusky nipples behind the lacey pink bra she wore made his mouth go dry. She was completely covered now.

That was good, right? No more heart shaped ass in the peek-a-boo briefs. No smooth ivory skin with its smattering of freckles. And no more luscious mounds covered in barely-there lace.

This was much better. Right?

Sad growl.

"Uh, yeah, sure. No worries," he grunted, finally responding.

"Thank you," she said.

Brayden looked up in time to see her cheeks redden with embarrassment. Biting her bottom lip, she waited, her hair curling around her shoulders, still damp from the snow outside.

Shit.

She was uncomfortable. What was he supposed to do now?

Say something, his Bear urged.

His inner beast was always angry with him lately but even more now for causing her any kind of disturbance.

"Uh, cute sweater."

"Thanks?"

For some reason that sounded like a question, but what did she want from him? He didn't do small talk. Jessica looked down at the green and red elf that seemed to be dancing across her breasts and shrugged.

He almost groaned aloud. The ugly Christmas sweater was anything but cute. Whatever. She always looked fucking great to him.

The material was loose over tight leggings, simple and comfy. But Brayden was treated to a peek of the tops of those luscious mounds when she tugged on her fuzzy, red-knit boots.

Not a particularly sexy ensemble, but after he'd briefly seen what lay hidden beneath, the outfit was hot as fuck.

The way that sweater hid what he now knew were larger than average breasts with pert nipples and supple skin made him want to take it right off her. And forget about those pants. Was it possible to be jealous of clothing?

The thin black material hugged her thighs and ass, leaving him with little to imagine except how sweet her hidden curves would feel beneath his hard body.

He loved a woman with a little extra something, and sweet Jessica had that for sure. She was shapely as a woman should be.

Neither man nor beast was attracted to a woman who looked more like a stick figure than full of flesh and blood. Brayden was a Bear who liked curves. And Jess had those in spades. Curves he'd love to get his paws on.

Fuck. No curves. Jess is off limits.

Yes. Curves. Mate, his Bear insisted.

"So," Jessica said, eyebrows raised.

"So," Brayden responded not so cleverly.

Dammit. Why the hell did she short-circuit his brain now of all times? Brayden wished he could leave the room and come back in again. But then he'd have missed seeing her sweet body.

And boom.

There went his cock again. Instant hard on.

"Uh…"

He knew he needed to say something, anything to keep things from getting any more awkward.

Thankfully, before things could get weirder between the two of them, he heard the sound of someone coming.

Great. More people to witness his idiocy. Maybe he could excuse himself now without looking like a coward for running away from the sweet she-Cat. Turning to see who approached with a smile, Brayden froze in place.

Shit.

He was stuck in the room for certain now. In walked the person he wanted to see least of all.

Uncle Uzzi Stregovich.

The magical matchmaking motherfucker who was there to ruin Brayden's damn life. Jess's face lit up, and Brayden frowned. Why was she so happy to see the old Witch?

"Uncle Uzzi! You're back! I am so glad to see

you," she gushed, running forward to embrace the bearded Witch.

"Hello again, my dear. You look lovely, yes," he replied, kissing her cheek.

And it was not until that moment that Brayden realized he'd been holding his breath. When he released it, the growl that expelled from his lips was intense, causing both Uzzi and Jess to back away from each other. Both Witch and Tiger stared at him for a moment before the old man clapped his hands.

"Well, this is going to be fun!" Uncle Uzzi announced.

His blue eyes were twinkling with glee and no small hint of magic. Jessica tucked her hair behind her ears, and Brayden just stood there.

Grrrrrr.

Chapter Five

"So, Beta Brayden Smith. And you, Jessica Maverick. What were you two doing when I walked in?" Uncle Uzzi asked with a sly smile as he entered the room.

"Just chatting," Jess replied in a rush.

"Well, I don't believe in accidents, and my liebling would say this is positively fortuitous," the Witch replied.

Hunter and Elissa walked in just after the enigmatic man. Hand in hand as usual, they greeted the older, and much shorter male Witch, with hugs and handshakes.

The ruling Alpha couple of the Maverick Pride were smiling, unable to take their eyes off each other. Their love story was something of a fairytale, the stuff of legends and immeasurable envy, he'd hazard a guess.

That kind of devotion was simply too good to be a common occurrence. Unattainable for anyone else, at least as far as Brayden was concerned.

His animal growled at him. He didn't like the insinuation that he would never have that kind of love. Not one little bit. The beast clawed at his skin in response, wanting out.

Brayden counted to ten in an effort to calm his Bear. It was nearly impossible. Especially when a picture of Jessica's scantily clad bottom flashed in his mind again. Was the image permanently burned inside his brain?

Yes, his Bear growled.

Fuck me, his human half returned.

Mate, the animal responded.

The thoughts were followed up by lusty thoughts and desires from his perverted Bear. The damn animal was positively drooling over the saucy redhead. He ground his teeth together as other members of the Pride shuffled in.

Most everyone greeted each other with nods or casual hellos. Even though the Barvale Clan he'd come from was small, the Maverick Pride was even smaller. They had far fewer numbers, but in a way, it was one of the things he liked about it.

Less drama that way. Or so he thought. Brayden cringed as some of the Pride's few females came in. These were the ones of an age to mate, and they had been invited by the Neta to attend this meeting. Less than half a dozen women, and each was dressed to the nines in clothing not at all suitable for the winter weather.

His gaze quickly passed over the flat-ironed hair and ridiculous high heels, unconsciously settling on the curvy little she-Cat who sat curled on one corner of the couch. She seemed to avoid the new arrivals.

Not that he could blame her. But for some reason, she also seemed to stay away from Elissa, whom he knew to be her friend.

Odd. And a little bit brave really.

Jessica was not hiding behind her brother's position in this room with her peers. The women eyed her and whispered to each other, laughing cattily. A fact that made his Bear snarl and stomp inside of him. They should know better than to mock the sister of the Pride Neta.

Where was all this protective bullshit coming

from? He had to wonder. Brayden's shoulders were starting to tense, and sweat was forming on his brow. His Bear did not like the tension in the room. Not one little bit.

Fuck.

He wished he could just walk out of the closed off living room, but that would be disrespecting his Neta. Brayden would never abide such a thing from anyone, especially not himself.

He'd just have to deal with it. And if he flashed those women an angry glance, purposely showing a little fang, enough so that one of them turned away and the others kept swallowing nervously, then that was fine with him. Especially, so long as it kept his beast calm.

"Okay, everyone, listen up. Uncle Uzzi here has graciously agreed to bestow his particular talents on our Pride. I want all of you to meet with him briefly over the next few days. He will be in town as our honored guest, staying in the Pride House. You will make yourselves available, and you will be agreeable to whatever Uncle Uzzi says. Is that clear?"

Shit.

Maybe Brayden should crack a window or something? Suddenly, he felt as if all the air had been sucked out of the room.

"Dude, you okay?"

Reg walked in a few minutes later, idling over to the big Black Bear.

The smaller, but still formidable Tiger Shifter gazed around the room. It might have been Brayden's imagination, but perhaps the younger male's eyes stopped to stare a moment longer on Jessica than necessary.

His Bear made his displeasure known by roaring so fucking loudly in his head he had to close his eyes to shut him up.

Mine.

Shit. There it was again. One word, loud and clear. Brayden did not like it. Not one little bit. Then his Bear said it again in a much louder, impossibly deeper voice.

MINE.

"Easy, dude. I meant no disrespect. I didn't realize it was like that," Reg replied with his gaze averted and his neck bared for the Beta.

Shit. Brayden paused, wondering who else had heard him.

"Did I say that out loud?"

"Say what? Dude, you are growling like you wanna take my fucking head off man. I'm sorry," Reg repeated, hands raised in surrender.

"I get it. I need to be more respectful of the Neta's family. Jess is just looking good is all," Reg replied, nodding in Jessica's direction.

Brayden had to work extremely hard not to punch the shit-eating grin off that asshole's face. Tigers loved to play fast and carefree, but Bear's did not buy into that. Words and actions had consequences. If Reg did not shut up soon, he was gonna learn that the hard way.

"Dude, you with her?' he asked, realization dawning on the younger male.

"What? No! It's not like that, but you'd do well to remember just who she is," Brayden countered sternly.

"Yeah, yeah. Got it. So, you won't mind if I-"

Reg didn't even get to finish his sentence before Brayden had the man by his throat. Fury and rage spread through him like wildfire. His animal outraged at the mere suggestion.

No one would be doing anything *to,* or *for,* or *with* Jessica.

No one but him.

"Uh, Brayden?"

When had Hunter walked to his side? The Bear could not be sure. He was too busy watching the color drain from Reg's face as the Tiger struggled to break free from his hold.

"Brayden?"

A little more force that time, but his Neta hadn't resorted to using his Alpha voice. Not yet. That meant Brayden didn't have to let go of his new favorite squeeze toy, right?

"Yes, Neta?"

He always was a polite cub. His mother said so. No reason to misplace his manners now.

"Put Reg down. Uh, please," Hunter said.

He'd added the last word after his mate elbowed him in the side. Elissa's scent was soothing to his Bear. The animal recognized the Nari. He wanted to protect and please her, as was his duty. But his inner Bear also wanted to punish this man who thought to covet what the animal now considered his.

"Hey Brayden."

"Nari," he replied calmly, ducking Reg's wild kicks easily.

"Why don't you put Reg down? Come on. Then we can go over here and chat with Uncle Uzzi? I, uh, made a fresh batch of honey oatmeal cookies," Elissa ventured in that smooth, yet commanding way she had.

Honey oatmeal cookies?

"Come now, everyone else is gone. It's just us. The rest of the Pride have been given their appointment cards and are waiting to be called," she said softly, lowering his arm with a gentle nudge that he would never oppose.

"Fuck, Brayden. What the hell?" gasped Reg from his new position lying flat on the floor.

Brayden did not care for his tone. He growled at the man who squeaked then ran out of the room.

"*Ha ha ha.* You made Reg squeak," Elissa said.

She giggled, and snorted, slapping a hand over her mouth. Her eyes were still alight with mischief, and Brayden figured he was not in all that much trouble.

"My love," Hunter said to his mate.

"You'll destroy the man's pride if you keep laughing at him."

"I'm sorry, Reg!" she called out, still chuckling.

This was the reason Brayden liked her so much. There was nothing fake about Elissa.

"So, Brayden, do you want to tell me what that was about?" Hunter asked him.

"Uh, no. Not really, Neta."

"Fine. You're up first, man. Uncle Uzzi is in the conference room waiting for you."

"Neta, with all due respect, I don't need help finding a ma---"

"Brayden, I know things were rough for you when you first joined our Pride. I know you have history, but I believe Uncle Uzzi can help ease your past hurts. He has done wonders for me and Elissa. We both want all of the Pride to be as happy as we are. The more happily mated couples we have, the stronger the Maverick Pride will be," Hunter said with a brisk nod.

"Do it for me, Brayden. Please?" Elissa chimed in.

Shit.

He didn't have a chance in hell of saying no to both of them. He respected the Alpha couple too much to go against them. Not that he thought Uncle Uzzi could help him find his fated mate.

The fact was, Brayden Smith knew exactly who his one true and fated mate was.

Jessica Maverick.

He'd only just realized it for certain. But there was still no way in hell, he was claiming Jessica as his own. His Bear let out a mournful bellow. But even his beast could not change his mind. Brayden refused to doom her to life with someone as broken as him.

After the tragedy of John's death followed by

Valerie's suicide, Brayden did not deserve happiness. Jessica was so sweet and pure. She was much better off without him.

Now he just had to be strong enough to stay away.

Sad growl.

Chapter Six

"Excuse me, Mr. Stregovich?"

Jessica snuck inside the conference room shortly after leaving the scene in the living room behind.

Whatever it was that had the Pride Beta wanting to strangle Reg was probably something she did not want to know about. Bad enough her she-Cat was ready to climb the big, burly Bear after his macho display.

Eeek!

All those muscles. Who could blame her? Brayden was built like an Olympian god, for fuck's sake.

To think he'd seen her almost naked moments

before had her heart skipping beats. Jessica was all Shifter, but she'd gotten some recessive gene or something that made her curvy and rounded where her peers were svelte and lean.

Embarrassment made her cheeks pink, especially since she'd caught Brayden checking out the Pride's own personal beyotch gang. Those skinny females gave Shifters a bad name.

She understood why Hunter invited them, he was their Neta. But she would never understand how they could sleep around with every male that whistled at them, then acted like she was the one with a problem.

Jessica did not have any issues with sex. Hell. She wished she was having some right now. And no, she did not play into the old double standard that women were whores and men cool when they slept around. She believed everyone should treat themselves with respect, whether male or female.

Sex was natural, and it was good, but that didn't mean she intended to pass herself around like a tray of crackers, for fuck's sake. She had tensed with the arrival of those women, wondering why those females even bothered to get appointment cards to see Uncle Uzzi.

Oh well. To hell with those women. They'd never paid Jessica any mind except to make nasty quips about her size. Even though they frequented her boutique, they still put her down.

Jessica's Closet was the name of her shop, and it was the best damn one in town. She was fluffy, but she had good taste.

Stylishly sexy with a dash of practicality.

That was her motto. Apparently being a shop owner meant Jessica couldn't scratch the eyes out of those two-faced she-Cats for all the times they'd hassled her. More's the pity. But Jessica had learned to grin and bear it.

And she did on the daily.

Sure, she had some money in a trust, but after using some of it as start up cash for her shop, she tucked the rest away, wanting to leave the rest for her future cubs. Cubs she wouldn't have if she didn't find a mate. Her Tiger pressed against her skin, the she-Cat eager to claim hers.

Chuff.

Her boutique meant a lot to her, especially since she recently expanded her reach with an online store. Things were looking good, and she was getting more and more orders every day.

Jessica's Closet was one of the few boutiques that

catered to both typical and larger body sizes. She had always been a bigger girl. And no, she didn't mean big boned.

Jessica was a Shifter. She liked food, and it showed. She had thick thighs, a sizeable ass, and one or three belly rolls. Not to mention big, heavy breasts. She owned it, though.

Fuck yeah, she did. Jess liked her body. No apologies. Why the fuck should she make one? Curvy girls rocked. Everyone knew thick thighs made great earmuffs. At least that was what her pjs said. Being a virgin, it was beyond her realm of expertise.

Anyway, this curvy girl one happened to like pretty things. She wanted clothes that made her feel feminine without shaming her body type. And she offered that to every bigger girl out there.

Jessica's Closet provided her with an outlet to help other big and small women alike find clothes to make them feel pretty, too.

She used to think her store was all she needed. But she was getting older now, and she wanted a mate. She'd finally realized after humiliating herself by running after Lance for the past few months. Her attempts at vamping him had yielded zero results, and while it had hurt at first, she was glad now.

The slightly younger Tiger was a straight up

playa. She was fine with his attitude about little or no stings stress relief sex. Wanted it herself, in fact. But he had too much respect for her brother, the Neta, to mess around with her.

She accepted the letdown gracefully. It wasn't like she'd offered herself to him, but it had been a near thing. Thankfully, he'd spared her the embarrassment very tactfully.

"You're not like the other women in the Pride, Jessicat. You're the Neta's sister. You're special. Someday, you will meet a great guy who will want nothing better than to kiss you silly for days on end. I just hope he's worthy of you."

Lance's words had resonated with her. Even after he'd patted her shoulder in a brotherly way and walked off.

That image of being kissed silly for days remained after she'd already dismissed the big Tiger. It was etched in her mind, a fantasy she could picture, but not really because, well, like with the rest of her body, her lips had been fairly unused.

Was it possible to receive kisses that could last for days? The idea had both her human and feline sides burning up with curiosity.

Prrrrrrrrrrr.

That was exactly what Jessica wanted.

A big, hunky man who desired her above all others. One who wanted to get to know her mind as well as her body. And most of all, who wanted to kiss her silly for days on end.

So yeah, she was technically twenty minutes early for her time slot with Uncle Uzzi. Since it didn't look like anyone was with the enigmatic Witch, she took a chance and walked into the room with a large dish of honey oatmeal cookies and chocolate caramel brownie bites courtesy of her Nari. Elissa was truly one hell of a cook.

"Come in dear, and please, call me Uncle Uzzi," the Male Witch smiled at Jessica and held out his hand.

It was warm and surprisingly strong. For a moment, she thought she felt a buzz where their palms had touched.

Uncle Uzzi was an older gentleman, but he was not fragile. He was a supernatural, a Witch, and despite the white beard and the slight crinkling at the corners of his sparkling blue eyes, he was power-ful. Flecks of light flickered throughout his gaze, signaling his Magic was joining them for this conversation.

Jessica ignored the little shocks she felt when Uncle Uzzi squeezed for just a moment. Her own Tiger crept forward, sniffing at the Witch before settling down. Her animal more than approved of Uncle Uzzi. The she-Cat was eager to be mated and claimed, and this was her best chance.

Prrrrrrr.

"My dear, you have the most unique teal colored eyes I have ever seen, tell me, does your Tiger have them as well?" Uncle Uzzi asked.

"Yes, actually," Jessica replied.

She felt herself blushing and sighed in resignation. It was not an attractive look on natural redheads, but she couldn't help it. Jess just did not get compliments often.

"Marvelous! Now, why are you here?"

"Well, I know it's not my turn yet-"

"That's alright. Looks like my first client is a little busy at the moment. So dating has been rough, huh?" he asked, and remarkably, she felt a connection with him.

"You have no idea. I mean, Hunter is a great brother, but he can be a little, well, a little, uh-"

"He's been *pussy-blocking* you, right?" Uncle Uzzi nodded knowingly.

"Um, what?" she asked, eyes wide with surprise.

"You are Tigers here? Felines? Pussycats, yes? And your Alpha male brother has been denying you some much needed sexy times, am I right? I believe *pussy-blocking* is the correct term," Uncle Uzzi smiled mischievously and bit into a brownie.

"Liebling, only one, I promise," he said to no one at all.

"It's my Betty. She looks out for me even in the beyond," he explained.

"Oh, I am so sorry," she began.

"Don't be. We had a wonderful life together, and I look forward to joining her in the next big adventure. Now, these are divine. That Elissa is an amazing chef," Uncle Uzzi said.

The Witch moaned happily and took another bite of his brownie. He wiped his mouth and hands on a napkin and took a sip of tea.

"Um, yeah, she is. And yes, you are right. No one will date me because of my brother. Even worse, Uncle Uzzi, um, no one will you know," she mumbled.

"Oh, you mean no one will have sex with you. So then you are a virgin, yes?"

"Shhh! Look, I am not technically a virgin, But I might as well be. Uncle Uzzi, I know I am not like the other women here. I don't look like the typical

Shifter. I'm too tall, I have a big stomach and jiggly thighs, but I'm not hideous or anything, right?"

"Of course not! Did someone say that?" he asked, aghast.

"No, well, some of the other women imply I'm fat when I see them, but I don't care what they say. The way I see it, those bitches are just *hangry*! Like eat a brownie and maybe you won't be such a bitch," Jessica snarled.

"Ha! That is hilarious," Uncle Uzzi wiped his eye, and continued.

"I am going to have to remember that one, dear. So tell me, how do you feel about sex?"

"Oh, Uncle Uzzi, I know nothing about it really. The first and *only* time I ever had sex was with some skinny little normal when I was away on a retreat in college. It lasted all of fifteen minutes, and it was pretty damn embarrassing. We hardly even kissed."

"That is unfortunate," he replied, concern in his sapphire gaze.

"I don't even remember the last time I've been on a real date," Jessica moaned.

She knew her face was on fire with humiliation, but she just couldn't hold back. Once she opened up, it was a flood of emotions and disappointments that just had to come out.

"Oh, my dear, that truly sucks. Now, I know we can do better than that for you. So, let me just get everything straight. You want a mate, but one with a high sex drive, right?"

Jessica knew she should be embarrassed, but her gaze narrowed. She felt herself nodding. It was true. She wanted sex. It was only natural, right? Why should she deny it then?

"Okay, so good sex is a must. I understand, any flesh and blood being would. But am I also right in guessing you want a mate to match your mind and heart to go with all the hot and sticky times?" Uncle Uzzi's eyes flashed as he gauged Jessica's answer.

"Yeah," Jessica said, exhaling deeply.

Suddenly, she knew sex for the sake of sex wouldn't be enough for her. She needed more than just a roll in the hay. She deserved more.

"Yes," she answered again, with more feeling this time.

"I want sex. I want soul-searing, passionate, dirty, messy, heart-stopping sex. But I want more than that, Uncle Uzzi. I want to be kissed."

"Now I know that man you took to bed in college didn't know what he was doing, because kisses usually do occur before and during sex."

"I know, Uncle Uzzi, and he tried," she said with a snort.

"But I want real kisses," she emphasized.

"Deep, long, passionate kisses that make me breathless and last for days on end. Kisses that touch me inside, and leave my toes permanently curled."

"Wow. My dear, it sounds like you've given that a lot of thought," Uncle Uzzi replied gently.

"I have, and I know what I want."

"What do you want, Jessica?"

"I want to feel special. To be loved in every way. I want to be kissed, Uncle Uzzi, like the way I described, by a man who wants to be with me. I think you are right, I want a mate."

"Excellent," purred Uncle Uzzi, but his attention was behind Jessica's head.

Tingles danced up and down her spine. Eyes wide, Jessica turned to see what, or rather, *who* the older Witch was staring at.

No. Fucking. Way.

Jessica could have died right then and there. Turned out, her private conversation with Uncle Uzzi was not so private. In fact, it had attracted an unexpected pair of ears.

Very big, very sexy ears.

Fuck me.

She froze.

"Ah, Brayden Smith," called Uncle Uzzi.

"Why don't you stop hovering near the door and come on in here? Take a seat next to our lovely Jessica."

Prrrrrrrrrrrrrrr.

Chapter Seven

Grrrrooooowwwlllll.

The Black Bear who'd always lived inside of Brayden seemed to grow larger in that metaphysical plane where he waited to be called. So intense was the feeling running through the beast that Brayden could hardly move.

The second he'd heard Jessica's voice, he knew he should have turned around to leave. Her pull was rivaling gravity, and it was all he could do not to run inside and scoop her up in his arms.

Hell.

Turn, walk, run, but he remained frozen in place. Something powerful, indescribable, kept him rooted to the spot. Without any other recourse, and much like an eavesdropping dickhead, he'd stayed, and he'd listened.

Fuck, how he listened.

Comprehension still eluded him as the seductive tone of her voice wrapped around Brayden's body like an invisible lead, tugging him forward. At first, it was just mild curiosity, but the more she spoke, the worse it got.

His Bear pushed and scratched against his skin, urging him to move in closer to the sexy as hell woman who was becoming more and more important to his animal.

The mention of a former lover had his Bear near to bursting free. A wave of pure jealousy flowed over him so fast it left him short of breath. If not for the explanation that followed, he might've done some serious damage to the room at large. As it was, he'd only managed to crush the doorknob in his hand.

Shit.

He'd have to replace that. But that was not important. Only his mate mattered. And right then, she was upset.

That was not okay with him. Maybe he could still hunt down that asshole who'd taken her virginity and beat some sense into him. Didn't the soon-to-be-dead asshat know how to treat a woman?

And what about the rest of the idiot Pride? Was every Tiger in the vicinity a fucking moron? How could this gorgeous creature not know how truly lovely and desirable she was?

If he did not already spend so much time working with them, he might have been surprised. But it was a fact. All the men in the Pride were completely fucking stupid. And for that reason alone, he would let them live.

Fact was, Brayden was profoundly glad they were all tasteless morons. If they had paid more attention than was necessary to sweet Jessica, his Bear would likely demand he round them up and teach them a lesson.

Actually, that sounded good to the animal either way.

Grrrrrrr.

Mine.

No one looks.

No one touches.

No one but me.

The sound of his name brought his head up and immediately he was taken in by a pair of shocked teal eyes. Uncle Uzzi was grinning like the sly old Witch he was, but Jessica looked downright stunned.

Uh oh.

Brayden had been caught in the act of spying on the Neta's sister. Surely, there was some punishment involved. He only hoped she'd be the one to dish it out.

Images of Jessica and some handcuffs came to mind, and while it wasn't necessarily his kink, he could so get into that with her.

Grrrrr.

Fuck. He needed to get his mind out of the gutter.

"Brayden Smith," Uncle Uzzi repeated his name.

"Why don't you stop hovering near the door and come on in here? Take a seat next to our lovely Jessica."

Not ours. Mine, growled his Bear.

Brayden just ignored the animal and took a seat on the other side of the table. He did not trust himself to be close to Jessica at that moment.

He nodded his head in lieu of a verbal greeting, afraid to speak until he got his Bear more firmly under control. The facts that his fingernails had grown in length and darkened in color, and his arms now bore a dark smattering of fur, left little doubt that he was almost out of control.

"Should I go?' asked Jessica.

"No!" Brayden exclaimed.

The word had left his mouth before he could rethink it. He winced and shook his head. Dammit, he was going to fuck this up already, wasn't he?

"Well, kids," Uncle Uzzi said and smiled.

"This is going to be easier than I thought. As you know, your Neta has asked me to help strengthen your Pride by finding mates for all eligible members. But here you two are, and I didn't even have to leave the Pride House!"

"Oh, I don't think---"

"We're not---"

But even a half-assed denial refused to leave Brayden's mouth. The temperature in the room was boiling. His pants were too tight. Shirt too rough. Fuck. He really wanted to go for a walk through the woods in his fur to calm his inner beast down.

"Children," Uncle Uzzi said, eyeing them both and daring them to disagree.

"You two have been dancing around each other for quite some time now if I am not mistaken. And unless my dearly departed wife, Betty, is the one correcting me, I am very rarely mistaken," he said, his blue eyes still twinkling.

"So, this is what I am recommending. Go on a date. Together. Today. Now in fact," the old Witch commanded.

"But I have work," Brayden began.

A date? How could the old cook have come up with such a crazy plan so fast? His head turned, and he caught Jessica's stricken look.

Fucking hell. His Bear snarled at him, and Brayden opened and closed his mouth, trying to fix the damage he just did.

If he said no, she would think he wasn't interested in her. Nothing could be further from the truth, but with his past, maybe she was better off without him. Then the next thought came rolling into his head, and Brayden growled out loud, causing two sets of eyes to bore into him.

If he refused, Jessica would find someone else. Another male to wine her and dine her, kiss her, and stroke her, touch that sweet body, and claim her as mate.

Grrr.

If that happened, his Bear actually would go completely fucking nuts. He couldn't have that. Whether he was willing to take her as mate right now no longer mattered.

Ready or not, Braden's fated mate was sitting right there.

Mine.

"Jessica?"

"Yes, Brayden?"

Her head was turned away from him, and he didn't like that, not one bit. He waited a beat, willing her to look at him. What was it they always said?

Curiosity killed the cat.

But no, never that. His beast would not allow it. Still, she must have felt something like that, since one minute later, those electric teal eyes of hers landed on him, a questioning look gracing her beautiful face.

"Would you like to go out? With me?" he asked, feeling like a fucking cub.

But the second the words were out, his bear chuffed. The beast was finally happy he'd taken the step forward.

"Really?"

Braden could not believe how clumsily he'd asked her out. He was sweating by then, and so nervous, he damn near forgot to breathe. But the way her face lit up with joy and wonder had his pulse racing and thunder roaring in his ears.

So beautiful.

So mine.

Maybe this was not such a bad idea. Maybe she felt the same pull toward him he'd always felt toward her. If that were true, there were just so many possibilities in how this thing would play out. The only question was, was Brayden brave enough to take the chance?

"Yeah, really," he replied, and didn't even bother fighting his grin.

"Excellent!" Uncle Uzzi exclaimed.

"Now, I only have till six tonight, so if you two could please send in the next pussy?"

Brayden turned confused eyes on Uncle Uzzi, only to be distracted by the sound of Jessica's laughter.

Holy shit.

The sound was positively dazzling. Not to mention the way her face lit up. Jessica's coloring was just incredible. It fascinated him, from the bright teal of her eyes to the multifaceted reds in her mostly auburn hair. All of it complemented by dusky rose lips, a pert nose, stubborn chin, and the prettiest damn eyelashes he had ever seen.

He fucking loved watching her giggle. Wondered if she was ticklish, too. Hell, he could even picture running his fingertips along the soft skin of her stomach and sides. Of course, anytime he pictured that, his cock would start to swell, and it was back to reciting multiplication tables.

"Uncle Uzzi calls all Big Cat Shifters pussies,"

Jessica explained, wiping tears of mirth from her eyes.

"I see," Brayden replied, a smile tugging at his lips as he watched her.

"Thank you. I'm going to excuse myself to the ladies' room, but I will be in the hallway so we can talk. Okay?"

Jessica turned and hugged Uncle Uzzi, before retreating. Brayden was about to follow when the old Witch stopped him.

"Oh, and one more thing, Bear."

"Yes?"

"You better treat her right, or I will be seeing you again under less jovial circumstances, Mr. Smith," Uncle Uzzi promised with a glint of gold in his blue gaze.

"I will always treat Jessica right," Brayden said.

His Bear did not like challenges, but he recognized power in the old male, and he appreciated him using it on behalf of Jessica. Uzzi Stregovich was a magical matchmaker unparalleled in the supernatural world. His reputation preceded him, but Brayden was pleased to know he was a good man on top of that. He nodded at the old Witch before following Jessica's path to the other room.

The female was walking towards him, having

finished with the restroom, or so he assumed. She smiled, and he gestured in front of him. Together, they made it to the kitchen, but the place was packed with Tigers.

Brayden didn't want to have this discussion in front of an audience. He made sure to make eye contact with Jessica, then nodded towards the front of the house. After a minute, she followed him onto the nearly empty porch.

Fucking pussies.

His Bear chuffed. The animal could really get used to Uncle Uzzi's nickname for his fellow Pride mates. Rubbing a big hand along the back of his neck, he turned his head from side to side, looking for a more private spot. Brayden wanted to be alone when he said what he had to say.

"So, where do you want to go?" Jessica asked shyly.

Her cheeks were a pretty shade of pink, and her breath was coming out in little white puffs. Frowning, he realized he'd dragged her outside with no coat.

"Uh, are you cold?"

"No, I'm not cold," she replied.

Jessica raised her eyebrows, waiting for him to answer her first question.

"I know Uncle Uzzi seems to think we could be a couple, but uh, I have a past, Jessica."

"I know. I'm so sorry, Brayden," she replied.

There was so much sympathy clear on her face, his chest squeezed.

The female was always so sweet and kind. She was young and green, full of sunshine and life, like the promise of a spring day in the dead of winter.

Brayden was going to hurt her. His heart too closed off, his soul too broken. If he claimed her as his Bear wanted to, chances were he was going to ruin it. He knew it, and it was killing him.

The truth was Jessica Maverick deserved so much better than a broken Bear like him.

"Look, Jess, I was only going to talk to Uncle Uzzi because Hunter ordered it. I wasn't looking for a mate. I can't do permanent. It's not you---"

"Oh, uh, I see."

Jessica's voice went brittle and her spine ramrod straight.

"You don't have to explain yourself, Brayden, I understand. I know I'm not what most Shifters see as a desirable mate. And I don't blame you. Not really, but uh, if you could just excuse me," she said, and moved to go around him.

Brayden held his arms wide, preventing her from

leaving. He needed to explain to her that she'd gotten it all wrong. There was not a fucking thing wrong with the woman! Didn't she know that?

Grrrr.

His Bear tore into him, and he allowed it. Brayden deserved to feel the pain inflicted by his angry beast. Even when he tried not to, he'd fucked up and hurt her anyway.

This was not how he'd planned for this conversation to go. He was simply going to---

You were going to what? Tell our mate she was not what we wanted?

His Bear pushed the words into his head, roaring his fury inside his mind. The animal clawed at his insides, enraged with him for fucking this up.

"Get out of my way," she said, refusing to look at him.

"Just give me a second, please, Jess. That is not what I meant to say."

"I know you were already mated, Brayden. I heard the story, and you have my deepest apologies," she said, eyes brimming with tears.

"Maybe you've found your true love once, and don't believe it can happen again. I get that. I really do, and look, I am sorry if Uncle Uzzi put you in an awkward situation---"

"No, that's not it," he growled, and ran a hand over his face.

His beard had already doubled in length, though he'd trimmed it that morning. No doubt it was due to the tension he was feeling. Being a Shifter was complicated.

"Let me take you out to lunch," he surprised himself by saying.

"I mean if you want to. But I would really love the chance to explain myself without sticking my foot in my mouth," he added with what he hoped was a tempting grin.

He held his breath, waiting for her to reply. So much hinged on the next word that would fall from her plump pink lips.

Shit. How had this happened so suddenly? When did his future happiness depend on one woman?

Uzzi Stregovich was one powerful fucking Witch. Had he bespelled the Bear? Or maybe the truth had been right in front of him for years, and his inner beast was just tired of waiting for him to figure it out.

Ya think? growled the Bear inside his mind's eye.

Brayden could see the big animal rolling his eyes and covering his face with his paws. It was long past time to admit his feelings. Truth was, Brayden had been curious about the beautiful She-Cat for a while now. How could he not be?

Just look at her, he told himself.

She was gorgeous. Warmhearted and sweet. Not to mention sexy as hell. No wonder he wanted her like mad. And if Uncle Uzzi was to be believed, this incredible little Tiger wanted him too.

Fated mates were rare and wonderful in the supernatural world. Everything inside him was buzzing with energy at the prospect that she, Jessica Maverick, was destined to be his.

Mine.

Not yet, big guy.

He reined in his Bear and stood with baited-breath while Jessica bit her lip and weighed her decision to give him another chance. His pulse raced, heart pounded, and breath became jerky as his eyes remained glued to her sweet face.

One glance down at her body in the silly yet clingy sweater and skintight leggings had his cock throbbing with need.

Oh yeah. He had it bad. Maybe having a mate would be a good thing. And not just to strengthen the Pride, but to heal his wounded heart. Maybe Jessica Maverick would be good for him.

He just had to convince her to give him a chance

while proving to both himself and the Tiger that *this* was worth a shot.

"Well, Jess? What do you say?"

After another pregnant pause, she lifted her incredible teal eyes to him and, once again, he was struck by her beauty. The background was mostly gray and white. Winter in New Jersey was pretty monotone, if not for the deep wooden structure that was the Pride House and the rich greens of the pine trees in the woods behind them. But none of that could hold a candle to the fiery redhead with the teal eyes.

She positively glowed. Dazzling him with the reds and golds in her hair, and that icy teal gaze that sent shivers down his spine.

"Alright," she said.

But Brayden still didn't move. Not sure he heard her right.

"I'll go to lunch with you," she reiterated.

Brayden had no idea just how much hope he'd had pinned on her saying yes until she did. Then his Bear bellowed in triumph and his heart beat double time.

The slightest hint of a smile started slowly on her sweet face, and it was all he could do to stop himself from picking her up and throwing her over his shoulder like a cave-Bear.

"Yes? I mean, uh, yeah, good," he added in a softer tone of voice.

Was he ever going to act normal around her? Before he could answer his own question, Jessica laughed. A real belly rumbling sort of sound that he liked. A whole fucking lot. And Brayden had the answer to his own question.

He would make an ass of himself repeatedly just to hear that sound. A happy Jessica Maverick meant a happy Bear. Brayden never felt so good as he did, seeing her smile because of his idiocy.

So yeah, if he had to be a clown, he would. For her. Shit. This was real. His heart thudded, blood boiled, and body tensed. Brayden was dumbstruck staring at her, red hair dancing in the breeze like flames on a bonfire.

Mine, his Bear pushed at him, and for once, his human side did not fight it.

"So, later then, right?"

"Yes," he agreed.

Jessica stood there a moment longer, looking like the sweetest damn temptation he had ever seen. Possessive instincts he never knew he had rose like the tide as he simply took her in.

Her skin was smooth and clear, a peachy sort of

pale that made him think of sweet cream and sliced fruit. His Bear's favorite treat. But he had a feeling it was about to be replaced by something much, much sweeter.

Mate.

Chapter Eight

Jessica arrived at her boutique just in time to field calls and prep online orders.

It had been a mad rush that morning for whatever reason. Though Jess figured it was due to a certain white haired Witch setting up dates left and right.

Kylie, a young female Tiger who helped manage the store while working on her own designs, was so glad to see her, the woman tackle-hugged Jess.

"It's been insanity here all morning!"

"That's good, right? I am sorry I'm late, I uh, had a meeting," Jessica replied.

"OMG! You went to see him, didn't you?"

"Who?"

"That matchmaking Witch everyone is talking about! Well," the she-Tiger prompted.

"Who did he set you up with? Not Lance, right? That guy is so conceited!"

Jessica laughed and the two young college girls she'd hired part time walked in, not even looking up from their phones. She told them what needed doing and took Kylie's arm, pulling the woman to the back of the store. She didn't need everyone knowing her business.

"Oh, and by the way, I need more of those pink and white polka dot gift boxes. You said you would give me the email addy for your supplier? But first, spill," Kylie added.

Jessica sucked in a deep breath. This was all so new, she wasn't sure she wanted to tell anyone just yet. But Kylie wasn't just her store's manager and brilliant lingerie designer.

She was her friend. The blonde was a Shifter, and like Jess, she had curves on her curves while being a head shorter than most. Her designs were incredible. She made panties, bras, teddies, and all sorts of sexy gear and accessories that Jess sold in her shop.

She just loved her designs. Jessica knew good quality, and she had an excellent eye. She'd been toying with the idea of investing in *Kisses by Kylie,* which was the blonde she-Cat's label, and now more than ever she was ready.

Jessica already found an excellent manufacturer who was keen to get their hands on some of Kylie's prototypes. She was still deciding which to send first so they could be duplicated to sell in the store.

Right now, she had some basic panties and bras, and they were already some of her biggest sellers. The fact that Kylie was also a fluffier woman, like Jess, was a bonus.

All her designs came in real people sizes. They were comfortable, sexy, and wouldn't break the bank. Perfect for the type of attire *Jessica's Closet* was known for.

"First, thanks for working late today," Jessica said.

She had been out later than expected. After receiving an impromptu lunch invitation from the Pride Beta, she lost track of time. Being out on a date with Brayden had been easier than she'd expected.

"No worries. It was slow in the morning, but that just meant I could work on designs. The afternoon traffic made up for it though, and we sold out of those stretchy velveteen dresses you ordered on a whim. Anyway, look what I made," Kylie said and held up a silvery lace number that made Jessica's eyes bulge out of her head.

"Holy shit, Ky. That is gorgeous," she exclaimed.

"Thanks! I really appreciate you helping me and taking the chance on my work, Jess."

"Are you kidding? These pieces are fabulous! I was going to wait to tell you as a Christmas bonus, but I am so investing in your *Kisses By Kylie*. I already put in a call to my lawyer and financial advisor. I should have a proposal for you Monday."

"Oh my gods! Really? I mean, I have no idea how to start this. I only just moved here and don't have a lawyer---"

"Look, I would be dumb not to invest in you when you are so obviously a genius. And I already told Hunter to call the Pride lawyer on your behalf. His services are for everyone in the Pride. You can meet with him at your convenience, and he will help you with my offer and any counter offers you might make. Then he can draw up a contract, so we are both protected."

"OMG! I am stunned, really!"

"Honestly, Ky, this is gonna be awesome. You are really gonna start building your brand, and I will just be lucky to get to sell you before you get bought up by some crazy big department stores," Jess said and laughed as her friend tackled her again.

"I am so happy, Jess, thank you."

Kylie jumped up and down in her excitement.

"Listen, I am so into this, but I don't want to sell out to some big corporation. At least, not yet. I am thinking, I can start that affiliate program you talked about and other small boutique owners like you can sell *Kisses by Kylie* too."

"Sounds amazing," Jessica replied, excited for her friend.

"You think so?"

Kylie sounded so elated, and Jess was thrilled for her. It was a good move. Jessica was happy to help. She always thought money should work for the person who had it, and she hardly had to do anything here at all.

It would be work, of course, and she would make sure Kylie was not being taken advantage of. The woman was too kindhearted sometimes. But ever since she came to town, Jessica had a good feeling about her. She had a past, something about her old Pride, but she was safe in Maverick Point under the Neta's protection.

The two females had hit it off immediately, and Jess even offered her a place to stay. Now, Kylie lived over the shop in the tiny attic apartment above Jessica's. The three story building was just the thing she'd wanted when she'd returned from college. Lucky for her to have an inheritance that allowed her to buy the property without any issues.

"Of course, I think this is awesome," Jessica replied, answering Kylie's whispered question.

She ran her hands over the silver silk and lace confection the designer still held, wondering if a certain Bear would like something like that or if he were more a cotton panty sort of guy.

Not that she would be finding out anytime soon. Or would she?

Ugh.

Damn the man for confusing her so.

"Alright, what went down with you today? You seem up one minute and down the next. Come on. Spill!" Kylie demanded for the second time.

She was a pretty woman with her short blonde curls and big green eyes. She'd moved to Maverick Point after spotting their own little mountain in her rearview mirror. Jessica loved hearing that story.

The she-Tiger had left her old Pride and was driving across the country, looking for a place to start over after she'd finished her first design course at a community college back in South Carolina.

Jessica had found her just a half mile out of town with a flat tire and brought her to see Hunter immediately. Ever since then, they'd been friends, and the woman had never looked back. Which was fine with Jess. She could not picture life without her.

"Fine," she said, knowing Kylie was like a Tiger with a bone when it came to wanting information.

"I went on a date."

"Shut up!" she gasped aloud. "OMG. Tell me more, girl," screeched Kylie.

Her cute little Southern twang made itself known in her excitement, and Jess grinned. Her excitement was positively contagious.

"It's no big deal. I mean yeah, I visited Uncle Uzzi, you know the Witch who runs the match-making service. He was at the Pride House today as you know, and don't think we won't talk about why you skipped it, anyway, he sort of suggested Brayden ask me out," she explained hastily.

Jessica felt Kylie's eyes boring into her with curiosity. She looked down, pretending to study her cuticles, and felt her cheeks burning under her friend's scrutiny.

"Wait? How did she know you had the hots for Brayden?"

"What do you mean? I don't have the hots for Brayden," Jessica replied, and the stink of her lie burned her own nose hairs.

Uh oh.

Okay, fine. Maybe she had the hots for a certain sexy Bear. Her inner Tiger chuffed, and she rolled her eyes. The silly feline had more than the hots for the big sexy Bear. She wanted to rub her scent all over him, roll over on all fours so he could mount her, and get started making cubs.

Eeeeek!

Prrrrrrr.

"Fine. Maybe I am sort of attracted to him," She admitted under Kylie's emerald stare.

"Look, I didn't even realize it until today," Jessica said and shrugged, new hurt winding its way through her veins.

"Not that it matters. He wants to be *friends*."

"What? Oh that is some *toro excretio*," Kylie replied, using the Latin for bullshit.

"I'll be fine, Ky," Jess started.

"No way. Let's finish locking the doors, then we can head upstairs for some margs and snacks. I got just the tequila to make you start talking, girl, and you are gonna tell me everything," Kylie said, nodding and squinting her eyes at Jess.

All those Southern no nonsense mannerisms she had made Jess smile despite the heartache. She was right. Jessica could use some girl time.

A little while later, both women were in Kylie's

apartment, since she wanted to show Jess more of her new samples. And she was the one with the tequila.

"Is this spiked?" Jessica asked.

"Just a little *magibrew* added. I don't want us sauced, but let's face it. We need to let our hair down," Kylie said.

Jess had made a pit stop at her apartment, where she grabbed a little tray of cheese cubes, rosemary crackers, sliced salami, and slivers of fresh jalapeno peppers. A perfect snack to go with some classic margaritas and girl talk.

It had taken them an hour to close up the store and was now nearing six o'clock. Tequila, snacks, and some girl time were a perfect way to end what had been, in all honesty, a really confusing day.

"Okay, start at the beginning," Kylie instructed, popping a loaded cracker in her mouth.

She was a good friend. Kind and honest. Much nicer than many of the other she-Cats who'd come running to the Pride House earlier that day to meet the famous matchmaker.

If only Jessica could have been a fly on the wall during those meetings. From what Elissa had told her, the women had not been thrilled with Uncle Uzzi's advice. The old Witch had told the other females they'd needed to grow as people before they thought about getting mates.

The very idea made Jessica chuckle, and she made a mental note to send the elderly Witch a box of Elissa's brownies as thanks.

"So, after that whole awkwardness, what then?" Kylie asked.

"Well, he took me to this really good sushi restaurant in Maccon City. It's called *Roll Over*."

"That's like a two hour drive, isn't it?" Kylie asked with a mouthful of cheese, so it sounded more like *thatliketwoourdriveinnit*.

Good thing Jessica spoke fluent *girl-with-food-in-mouth*.

"Yeah, and with traffic, it took longer."

"So, what did you do on the way?"

"We talked."

"You talked?"

"What else could we do while he was driving, you pervert?"

Jessica tossed a cracker at Kylie, but she just caught it and giggled as she shoved it in her mouth.

"It's crazy, but I never really had a conversation with him before. Did you know male Black Bears in the wild weigh about five to six-hundred pounds and Shifters are almost double that? His Bear is over nine hundred pounds," Jessica said.

"That's really interesting and all, but did he, you know?"

Kylie waggled her eyebrows. The blonde knew all about Jessica's obsession with the perfect kiss. They'd shared many a bottle of tequila with Jess describing her ideal mate in detail. Silly really, but a girl had to dream.

"No. That's why I am so frustrated. He wanted to kiss me. I mean, I think he did. I could scent his desire, but he pulled back last minute."

"Okay, hold up. You need to go over every move he made from the time you sat down to eat."

Jessica sighed. She supposed Kylie was right. So, taking a huge gulp of her delicious classic marg in the stemless glass with black salt clinging to the rim, Jessica recanted her entire date.

"What do you feel like having?" Brayden asked.

"Want to share one of those big boats?"

She'd meant it innocently enough. They were Shifters, and they could eat, but the second she found the item on the menu, Jessica's cheeks had heated furiously.

"You mean a 'love boat'?"

"Um, yeah, I guess. Sorry. If you don't want to-"

"No, it sounds good," he insisted and placed their order.

"You ordered the LOVE BOAT!"

Kylie snickered, interrupting the story by belting out the old television show tune. Off key of course.

"That was a Freudian slip if I ever head one," the Southern Cat added unhelpfully.

"*Shyaddap*," Jessica retorted and playfully pushed her aside.

"Look, I forgot what it was called. Anyway, we got it and it was delicious. By the time we'd eaten everything, including some green tea ice cream for dessert, we'd been there over an hour."

"Okay, then what happened?"

"Well…" Jessica began, falling back into her story.

Brayden held Jessica's hand and walked her to the car.

"I really enjoyed going out with you, Jessica."

"Thank you. I had a nice time, too."

"Maybe we can do this again sometime?"

"I'd like that."

Her stomach clenched as she smiled at him and waited. This was it. The moment she'd been dreaming about since she was a cub. Her purrfect kiss was imminent.

Brayden leaned in closer. So close, their breath

mingled. Jessica tipped her head back, eyes half-closed as she watched the near descent of his lips.

"Seat belt," he said, clearing his throat.

He'd spoken in a hushed tone, and it took a moment for her to understand the words. The sudden loud click of the buckle connecting separated them with a jolt, and she could have died from embarrassment.

Jessica smiled tightly, and Brayden moved to the driver's side.

"That was it? That was the near kiss?"

"Yeah. The rest of the trip we talked about nothing, really. Christmas, sports, music. Nothing big."

"Did he ask you out again?"

"Uh, no, actually," she murmured, looking into her near empty marg glass.

"Well, that doesn't mean anything," Kylie said encouragingly.

But Jessica didn't believe that. Lunch had been nice, but was it anything more than a pity date?

Ugh.

She wished she knew.

"Hey, let me show you the new nursing bra I was working on for the Nari."

Just like that, Kylie changed the subject, for which Jessica was eternally grateful. She didn't want to spend too much time thinking about what had happened or what had not happened between her and Brayden.

Her girly parts were screaming at her for not just taking the big man in hand, but she had never been that forward.

Could she even do something like that? Most Shifter's owned their sexuality with a natural sort of sultriness that she did not seem to possess. Maybe she was doomed to a sexless life.

After all, if Brayden was her mate, he would have wanted her, right? Felt desire for her, at least. Isn't that what all Shifters felt when they met their fated mates?

Maybe Brayden simply wasn't hers.

Mine.

Her she-Tiger growled the thought, pushing it into her head with strength. The thought of trying to find anyone else made the feline positively furious.

But still. Jessica had her doubts. Maybe the infamous magical matchmaker Uzzi Stregovich had gotten it wrong.

Sad chuff.

Chapter Nine

"Brayden?"

Hunter's voice seemed far away as Brayden mulled over his lunch date with Jessica. He thought it went well, except for the nearly mauling her in her seat part. Damn female was so tempting, but she deserved better than to be jumped in a parked car like some horny teenager.

Then there was his other problem. Idiot that he was, he'd forgotten to ask her out on a second date. And no, he did not get her number either.

Fucking moron.

"Brayden!"

The snapping of the Neta's fingers in his face soon brought him back to the present.

"Are you with us here, man?"

"Yeah. Sorry, Neta."

"Alright, as Lance here is the newest member of your crew, I'd like to see you give him more responsibility than he's been getting. Do you think you can handle that, Lance?"

The murmured *yes sir* had Brayden's eyes snapping up. He liked Lance, but he was aware that Jessica had had a crush on the Tiger only weeks ago.

Was that resolved? Did she still feel an attraction to the man who was not only her own species, but closer to her age?

Brayden was fifteen years her senior. He might not look like it, but that didn't lessen the age difference. She'd seemed unaffected by the news at lunch.

It wasn't odd for Shifters' lifespans to be supernaturally long. They maintained youthful appearances for many more years than the average normal, and it was typical to have couples a decade or two, or three apart. His own father was twenty-five years older than his mother.

"We won the bids on several more projects in the surrounding areas. One is the construction of a new shopping center," Hunter began, using his computer to send updated schedules to everyone present.

The crews used tablets and laptops to communicate and evaluate projects and goings ons. Everything was computer based these days, and lucky for Brayden, he was fairly tech savvy.

Sure, he'd rather be tearing up some concrete than typing on a delicate piece of machinery, but that was just him. Bear Shifter, go figure.

"Alright, that about sums it up. You guys can go. Except you, Brayden," Hunter said.

Shit.

He'd been so distracted with thoughts of Jessica, he hadn't been paying attention.

Should have kissed her, his Bear growled the words at him.

He'd wanted to. When he placed her in her seat after they'd eaten that delectable Sushi, he'd been so close to claiming her rosy lips. Then he'd remembered what she'd said about kissing.

"I want deep, long kisses that last for days. Kisses that touch me inside and leave my toes permanently curled. I want to feel special. To be loved in every way."

Now, Brayden had no doubt in his mind that once he started kissing Jessica, they'd both go up in flames. It was the way of fated mates. And she was his. A fact that only grew clearer with every passing second. Despite his past, Brayden was more than certain Jessica Maverick was his fated mate.

She was the only woman the universe had

created specifically for him. In turn, he was the only male for her. Shifters who claimed their fated mates were blessed by the universe in a way others could only dream about. And now that he recognized the truth, he could not justify squandering this chance at happiness for them both.

Brayden wanted her so badly, he was resigned to spending the next few weeks bent over trying to hide the constant erection he seemed to have developed. At least, until he felt she was ready to move forward. He wanted Jessica completely in control. Needed her to be okay with this mating before he claimed her.

Fuck.

His Bear was being a total dick about it. The beast was threatening to go on a rampage if he couldn't have her soon. Still, he had a shadow of a doubt, and that was all he needed to stop him in his tracks.

Pain from his beast had his Bear whimpering inside his mind's eyes. The idea of mating went against the vow he'd made after the tragedy of John and Valerie.

The deaths of both his childhood friends still tore a hole through him whenever he thought of their tragedy. But Jessica was not Valerie. And he was not John. Their story could be different.

Shit.

He was being a coward. Poor Jess. She was probably feeling all kinds of rejected right now. And it was his fault. He really needed to get his head out of his ass.

Grrrrr.

His Bear scratched against his skin, and he closed his eyes to calm the beast while Hunter shuffled some papers around and returned to the seat behind his desk. A Bear on a rampage was not a good thing.

"Brayden? You seem distracted. What's going on, man?"

"Yeah, sorry. Nothing, bro. I'm good."

"You sure? Cause I'm here if you need to talk," Hunter replied.

The Tiger was a great leader. Caring and wise, he was also loyal and honest. There was no other man Brayden could ever imagine filling his role as Neta. If there was ever an issue with one of his Pride, Hunter would be there in a flash. It was one reason he respected the man so greatly.

"Look, I have some things to discuss about Uzzi and what he will be doing here," Hunter began, and Brayden waited for it.

"I know you aren't a Tiger, but you have a coveted rank in this Pride. One you earned, and I would like to see you keep it," Hunter began.

Brayden respected the Neta so damn much, and he was proud of the position he held within the Maverick Pride. But that was only guaranteed until the next challenge or until his Bear went crazy. Unmated Shifters had that tendency. Not that it was a choice or anything. Shifters were simply not meant to be alone.

It was the reason people like Uzzi Stregovich and his Magical Matchmaking Service fared so well amongst their kind. Sometimes Shifters needed help to find their mates. And discovering one's *fated mate* was best. Uncle Uzzi's reputation for helping Shifters was unmatched.

They were lucky he wanted to help the Pride. A fated mate was like nothing else in the universe. It was the other half to a Shifter's soul. The one person in all the universe perfectly created to soothe the beast, calm the animal, and complete the human half as well.

"I asked Uncle Uzzi to help the Pride for many reasons. One is that numbers are low. Our Pride has not been particularly fruitful as of late, and that does not bode well."

"Yes, Neta," he answered.

"Uncle Uzzi is gifted, my friend. He helped me find my fated mate, and I really am hoping you will listen to his advice. I noticed your unease as of late. Allowing Uncle Uzzi to help you will ease your Bear. You know, fated mates give Shifters an anchor to their human side, as well as undeniable strength through their common matebond. It's not a bad deal," Hunter replied casually.

Brayden could not agree more. It was a myth to some. A dream for most. And a reality to precious few.

Was Jessica his fated mate and was he throwing away the only opportunity he would ever have at happiness?

"So, what did Uzzi say to you today? Did he set you up with someone?" Hunter asked.

"Um, sort of," Brayden replied.

Fuck. He forgot about this part of it for a moment. Jessica was Hunter's sister, and as the Pride Neta, he deserved to hear it from Brayden's lips. His Bear demanded it. Brayden could not pretend with his animal, or this man.

Only the truth would suffice.

"Well, did he set you up? Did you go out with her? Who is it, dude?"

"Um, yes, I went on a lunch date."

"That's great, bro. Who's the lucky girl?"

Hunter was grinning at him, but Brayden did not let his guard down. The man was the only Tiger in the Pack who could give Brayden's Bear a run for his money, and though he had no wish to grapple with the beast. He was about to drop a pretty big fucking bomb on the guy's head. Best to be prepared.

Standing up, Brayden braced himself as he leveled a stare at his Neta before promptly baring his throat and averting his gaze.

"The truth, Neta, is this," Brayden began, clearing his throat.

"Jessica is my fated mate."

Rrrrooooaaaaarrrrrrrr.

Chapter Ten

Jessica walked slowly among the aisles of her small boutique. *Jessica's Closet* was a dream come true for her. Her first real taste of independence after leaving the Pride House.

Of course, Hunter meant well, but her older brother could not help his dominant personality. He was the Neta. Born to rule. And well, she wasn't one to take orders so politely.

She loved her little shop. Catering to a small town meant facing a lot of challenges. At first, her brother didn't think her business would survive, but she'd easily proven him wrong. It was all about knowing your customers.

That and her aptitude for technology had helped her a great deal. She had an online storefront where she got a lot of out-of-town, even international, traf-fic. The fact was, she provided for a specific clientele.

Plus sized women were unfairly categorized in the fashion world. Larger-sized clothing was deemed unattractive, as were the women who wore it. It often meant older styled clothing, ugly prints, cheap fabrics, and terrible cuts.

But not at *Jessica's Closet*.

Being a big girl her entire life meant she'd had two options. Either adjust to the hideous clothes available to her in their small town or look for something better. She chose the latter.

What a wonderful choice that turned out to be! She hummed to herself as she ran the vacuum over the hardwood floor and let her thoughts wander. Combined with the noise the machine made, she didn't hear the bells over the front door jingle.

"Jessica! There you are. My, this store is just divine," Uzzi Stregovich walked inside the boutique.

The older man was carrying a few wrapped packages, his blue eyes twinkling as he looked around and his magic seemed to wrap around him like a cozy blanket. He wore a gray wool suit and a yellow scarf with a red rose pinned to his pocket. Of course, appearing out of the blue as he had, the male

Witch scared a yelp out of Jessica, who turned off the vacuum with a flick of a switch.

"Uncle Uzzi? What are you doing here?"

"I came to check on you, of course," he said, handing her a box of delicious smelling pastries from the nearby *Cookie Shop*.

"Do you have time for tea?"

"Sure, come to the back," she said, leading the way.

"Tell me, dear, what is going on with the salon next door?" Uzzi asked as he placed his things on the table and took the box of goodies to open.

"Oh, that was Mrs. Bowers' place. She moved to Florida a few months ago, and she's still looking for someone to take over her lease. I think Elissa's old roommate might be coming to check it out soon."

"Ah, that would be Gretchen. Yes, a good plan all in all," Uncle Uzzi murmured and accepted the cardboard cup of tea Jessica handed him.

"So, how did your date with that giant hunk of a Bear go?"

Uncle Uzzi sipped and grabbed a cookie while rapidly flicking through the pages of a catalogue had been using for inspiration on her website.

He stopped and looked at the ads featuring plus size lingerie, and his eyes flashed to the rack of prototypes made by Kylie. He sure was a strange, quirky man, but he had an honest way about him, and Jessica definitely liked the older Witch.

"Um, it was alright I guess," Jess replied and shrugged.

"Did you want to order something?" she asked when he stood up to handle some of the lingerie.

"What? Oh no, dear, without my liebling I am afraid my desire for encounters of the flesh has waned. But I have many clients who share a certain body type, and I would love to pass information on your store to them, if I may?"

"That would be wonderful," Jessica replied.

She slapped on her metaphorical business-woman's cap and went about grabbing a bag, loading it with some flyers, business cards, and discount codes for him to give to his clients.

"Thank you, dear," he said, smiling again.

"I believe all women should feel confident and proud of themselves. I see that you certainly do, Jessica Maverick. I mean you wear clothes so well," Uncle Uzzi said and eyed Jessica approvingly.

The she-Tiger felt the compliment down to her toes and smiled back. It had taken a little while for her to build her self-esteem to a place where she felt really good about herself, and she appreciated his notice.

"I like clothes and I refuse to be told what I can wear because society would rather see a woman starve herself than be real," Jessica said honestly.

"Yes, I agree."

"I mean, I am not advocating unhealthy lifestyles, but for some of us, this is as good as it will get. Why shouldn't we be comfortable and pretty too? Just because we have curves does not mean we have to dress horribly," she continued.

Style for Jessica meant comfort, quality, and cuteness! Today she wore a pair of dark, tight jeans with strategic rips across her knees and one right under her left butt cheek. She paired the butter soft denim with an off the shoulder ivory sweater that showed just the right amount of her ample cleavage without being too slutty to wear at work.

Rather than take away from her, the pale color flattered her fiery mane, which she wore brushed over one side and held in place by a pretty rhinestone clip. A pair of shearling lined flats completed the ensemble.

"I completely agree. Besides, you do know that most Shifter males prefer women with curves. I have been told they are the perfect foil for all the hardness of the males of the species. A little cushioning for all that pushing," he said, and she laughed.

"Am I saying that right?" Uncle Uzzi queried.

"Uh, close enough."

Jessica's face flamed as she tried to come up with a reply.

"These sets of undergarments are lovely. *Kisses by Kylie?* Who is this Kylie? I believe I am going to have to give your address to a few more clients than I expected," he remarked.

"Thank you so much. She is a member of the Pride."

"Mated?"

"No," Jessica said with a grin.

"I see. Well, I am quite serious about knowing people who would love what you've done here."

"Thank you so much," Jessica said, snapping out of her daze.

"Kylie is a new member of our Pride. She moved here from North Carolina and was actually really shy about meeting you."

"Oh, well, no worries. When she is ready, you can send her my information."

"I will. She's a terrific person. She lives just upstairs, and seriously, her designs are great. I am wearing one of the strapless bras and matching panties right now. I swear, Uncle Uzzi, it feels like I'm naked under my clothes," Jessica whispered conspiratorially.

"Ha ha. Good, yes. I love that you are able to chat with me like I am family, yes?"

"I'm sorry, is that too much info?"

"Not at all, dear. I am, after all, Uncle Uzzi. Plus, it is a great selling point. Every well-endowed woman wants her under garments to fit comfortably. I think between that, and of course the added sex appeal, make these designs amazing. You know, I think I will take a few more cards. Thank you. Now, tell me the truth about your date."

"Oh, Uncle Uzzi."

Jessica's face fell even as she loaded a few more cards, flyers, and postcards into Uncle Uzzi's bag.

"Look, I know you are good at your job, but maybe you made a mistake."

"It has happened, though rarely. But why do you think so, my dear?" Uncle Uzzi asked, his blue eyes twinkling with magic.

"It's no secret, I am into Brayden, but he is obviously not interested in me. It's been two days, and I haven't heard from him."

"Two days? Hmm. Well, I know from your brother they have been dealing with new projects and preparing for the trial with the Council of Shifters for that miserable wretch, Blake. Perhaps the Bear had been tied up in meetings? I think maybe you might give him some time, Jessica. But not too much," he replied, a teasing grin spread across his face at the last.

"Alright," she said.

"I guess I should follow your advice, but really, I understand if I am not what he wants in a mate."

"Listen to me now, Jessica Maverick," Uncle Uzzi said, his voice thick with what sounded like Eastern Europe in his accent.

"Sometimes a woman has to take the bull, or in this case, the Bear, by the horns. Look deep inside of yourself and decide if he is the one for you. DO not wait for him, because if he is your mate, then he is worth the risk. You think about that," Uncle Uzzi replied.

The old Witch squeezed her hand then stood up with his bag full of Jessica's cards and flyers. He dropped an air kiss beside her cheek and patted her arm before turning one last time.

"Now, I must go. My driver waits to take me back to the Pride House, but you can depend on my clients reaching out soon. Oh, look at the time. I am late already for my meeting with the Neta," Uncle Uzzi said, and huffed out a breath.

His magic sparked, and he gave Jess a small wink before he headed out the door. He'd moved so quickly, the Tiger Shifter could not even reply.

Jessica's head was spinning. She picked up a business card that must have dropped from the pile she'd given the Witch, and shivers of magic shot through her arm. Shaking the teal paper, she shook off the brush with Uzzi's magic and returned it to the pile on the counter.

Jessica's Closet was done entirely in shades of teal and silver. It was her own little homage to the Maverick family sigil, taken from the color of their eyes.

The unique teal was passed down from generation to generation. A strong trait the Mavericks were proud of. It was her best feature if she said so herself.

Looking around, she sighed wistfully. This place was her dream, her passion, and it was doing very well.

But just lately, she wanted more. Especially since big brother had found his fated mate in Elissa. The Nari was just amazing, and Jess could not be happier for her brother. He deserved that kind of fairytale love, the happily ever after, no holds barred, soul searing, passion that she had dreamed about since she was a cub.

The thing of it was Jessica wanted that too.

Home, family, mate, cubs.

It was a mantra her Tiger kept repeating in her mind. And what's more, she wanted a kiss. And not just any kiss. She wanted the kiss.

The perfect kiss.

A kiss that makes my Tiger purr.

The question was, was the big Bear the man to do it?

There was no denying the way her she-Cat stood at the ready whenever Brayden was near. The animal inside of her was definitely interested in the sexy Black Bear. The woman, however, always seemed to turn shy whenever she was within ten feet of him.

Until lunch the other day, the Cat reminded her.

True. At lunch she'd been poised, refined even. She told stories and a joke or two. Heck, she had even coaxed a smile from the typically solemn Beta.

Then there was the physical evidence. Her stomach flipped over, and her heart raced in his presence. When his fingers had grazed hers after she'd asked for a napkin, her entire body shuddered.

Moisture pooled between her thighs, and Jessica

could hardly breathe. His rugged good looks and incredible over the top muscles made her mouth water. There wasn't a damn thing wrong with the man. Well, except for one thing, and she might be nit-picking here, but it was a pretty big deal to her.

Brayden seemed all too able to resist her.

Sad chuff.

Maybe she should do something to entice him?

Like what?

She dismissed the idea as quickly as it entered her head. Jessica was not going to play games. If Brayden thought she was his mate, then he needed to let her know.

She walked to the backroom as Kylie came in to start her shift.

"Hey girl, I'm gonna sit in the front and work on designs between customers."

"Sounds good," she replied.

"Yay. My favorite kind of day," the she-Cat drawled pleasantly.

Next week, it would be different. Last-minute shoppers for the holidays would be cruising every store in town for little knickknacks and gifts.

After her first year in the business, she had an idea what most folks were searching for, and had prepared by ordering plenty of scented lotions, bath bombs, hair clips, silk scarves, candles, and the like.

She'd even gotten a few local romance authors to allow her to sell some of their books. Jessica always was a sucker for a good steamy romance novel.

And for the adventurous male shopper who dared stepped into the predominantly female boutique, Jessica prepped several gift bags to make shopping easier on them.

She took lingerie sets from her *Kisses by Kylie* collection and matched them with candles, massage oils, lotions, CDs, books, and other doohickeys. Then Jessica wrapped them in tissue paper in special silver foil boxes and topped them with teal bows and ribbons. On the outside of each box was a label with a picture of the inside and the size information.

The idea was to give the customer a way to buy their girlfriends, wives, or mates an exciting gift they might actually like instead of a toaster or, gods forbid, an exercise bike, this holiday season.

Some males seriously had a death wish, she mused after hearing horror stories of what some men bought their significant others. Pots and pans were great, but sometimes a gift needed to be personal. Jessica walked to the backroom and saw the packages Uzzi had come in with earlier sitting on the table.

Uh oh.

"Kylie? I'm going to the Pride House to deliver these to Uncle Uzzi while he is still there," she said, waving to Kylie.

"Sure thing, boss," the pretty She-Cat returned.

Jess nodded at her and headed out to her little white four-wheel drive. It was cold, but she was fine in just her sweater and jeans.

With any luck she'd run into her Bear at the Pride House. Maybe then she could get a read on him. See if he was really what she thought he was.

Mate.

Chapter Eleven

Brayden paced the yard behind the Pride House in Bear form. Even taking a long run through the woods did nothing to relieve the animal's stress. He loved the clean smell that winter brought to the land and the beast had marveled at running through the frost covered mountains, but he hadn't alleviated any excess of energy he'd been feeling.

The snow-covered trees always looked pristine against the dark gray skies of the early afternoon in this part of Burlington County. Usually, it would help to settle his anxious animal. But not today.

The Council of Shifters had come to get a final testimony for Hunter about Blake Segal, effectively closing the file on the former Beta. They were all better off without the infectious male. He seemed to breed unrest, and his taint was even more obvious now with him dead.

Hunter was working to restore the balance, but it would take time. Especially after learning from the Council that a rogue group of Tiger Shifters with a beef against the Pride was encroaching on their lands. Anger at the trespassers, Brayden had excused himself for a run.

The Council representative who'd passed on the information was a Cougar Shifter named Dakota Miles. Loners in the wild, Cougar Shifters typically lived in a Pride, but anyone who worked in the Council did so at the expense of leaving their group to become allied to all Shifters in spirit. At least, that was how it had been explained to Brayden.

Not that he would ever want such a life. It was bad enough when his best friend had died, and the male's mate had looked to Brayden for comfort.

Fuck.

He really needed to tell Jessica the truth about that. She probably had the wrong idea about what kind of Shifter Brayden really was, and that did not sit well with him at all.

The Cougar had left them with a warning not to take the rogues lightly. Whatever. Those Council reps never brought good news with them. He'd sat through enough of those meetings to know that much.

As the Maverick Pride Beta, he was privy to their meetings with the leader of the Pride. He'd never heard the term Neta before coming to Maverick Point. Not unusual since he was a Black Bear Shifter, and that term came from an old Bengal word meaning leader.

Appropriate, he supposed, but why not just say Alpha? He'd asked Hunter once, and the man had smiled. He then explained the pomp and circumstance of Tiger Shifter tradition stemming from his English and Bengali roots.

Brayden wasn't much of a history buff and the entire idea behind imperialism was a mindfuck he in no way wanted to get into. But now that he thought about it, he supposed it made sense that the Maverick's had English ancestry.

It was in Jessica's hair and skin tone, where Hunter had obviously gotten his slightly darker skin from his Bengali heritage. Those Maverick eyes however, those were an exotic mix of both sides of their heritage.

Both siblings had that unique teal color, but Jessica's were way more intense. Everything about her was more intense as far as Brayden was concerned. She called to him like no other.

Jess was so fucking beautiful. Nothing short of a dream personified. She was smart, funny, and had this amazing quality, like she didn't even know how sexy and beautiful she really was. It only made her that much more attractive to him.

Throughout their date, he kept getting little hints of her honey-ginger spiced scent. He practically drooled on the table like an idiot just imagining tasting her. He'd bet anything she'd be mouth numbingly sweet and spicy. Just like fresh gingerbread drizzled in honey. That was his favorite holiday treat.

Grrr.

Even his Bear wanted a taste. Brayden had wanted to kiss her then, but he'd frozen. He only hoped he hadn't waited too damn long to call her after their lunch date. She probably thought he wasn't interested.

Wasn't that a fucking joke?

There could be nothing farther from the truth. He was interested all right, but he was cautious. If Jessica rejected him, he would never recover.

Mate, his Bear chuffed.

It was definitely a big risk, but it was one he was willing to take. She was worth it.

Fuck yes.

The female was worth anything and everything he had to give. Yeah. He should have called her the day after they'd had lunch. Should have sent her roses or something.

He'd never intended for so much time to pass. At first, he'd told himself he was giving her much needed space and time to adjust to the idea of him dating her. Afterwards, Brayden's duties had kept him occupied.

Dating?

His Bear growled and stomped. The animal wanted to claim her as his mate. Sooner rather than later. He wasn't a teenager who needed dates to confirm whether he liked the girl.

She was made for him. His fated mate. There would be no one else for Brayden. Not ever.

Being this far away from her was agitating his Bear. Even a two-hour trek through the woods, running at a vigorous pace, did nothing to spend his big beast's excess energy. He snorted and pawed at the ground, a warning to the Tigers lurking close by their Beta was in no fucking mood.

A noise from the front of the house had his great

ursine head turning around suddenly. His Bear snorted and stilled. He sniffed the air, and a rumbling growl filled his chest. It grew deeper and louder, shaking the very air as waves of nutmeg, honey, and ginger greeted his supernaturally enhanced nostrils.

Mine.

He tried to stop himself, but the Bear was harder to control in this form. He charged. The beast raced to the front of the house, just in time to see Jessica bent over her vehicle with that motherfucker Reg, standing a little too close for comfort. Mainly, the Tiger's comfort.

Grrr.

Jessica was practically tipped over, reaching into the trunk of her little SUV. Ass up in the air, wiggling from side to side as she attempted to retrieve whatever it was inside the vehicle.

Brayden's Bear purred at the sight. And what a fucking view it was. Her heart shaped ass was squeezed into a pair of jeans so tight they looked like she was poured into them. There was a slit right below her left ass cheek that left her soft, pale skin exposed to the elements.

Then he noticed the soon-to-be-dead Tiger grinning in that general direction. Was that dickhead really checking out Brayden's mate's ass? And in front of him, too.

Fucking Reg. Did the man have a death wish?

Possessiveness he didn't even know he felt welled up inside of him. Brayden growled deep in his chest, just loud enough for the man to hear him. A predator recognized another, and Reg's face paled as he turned his eyes on the Bear.

Brayden bared his fangs at the Tiger Shifter. He did not want to hurt Reg, but he needed him to understand Jessica was off fucking limits. He must have gotten the message cause the man swiftly backed up. Arms raised and gaze averted, he took the stairs two at a time, calling out a hasty goodbye to Jessica.

Good thing she was too busy to answer, gathering whatever had her sweet ass practically exposed for him. His chest rumbled as he watched her. The animal content to be near.

She seemed to have difficulty getting something and concern had him stepping forward, but not before the front door opened. That fucker had come back. Reg opened his mouth to speak, but this time Brayden widened his jaw, saliva dripping from his long, sharp fangs.

The Tiger male squeaked and shut the door. His

Bear snorted. He was really growing to like that particular sound from the man. Though the likelihood of him remaining capable of any sound would be highly diminished if he insisted on ogling Jessica.

Mine.

Okay, so the Bear needed a chill pill.

Not happening.

At least, not until he'd made her his. Jessica groaned with effort, and he found the noise irresistible. He moved forward and pressed his nose against her backside, unable to control the beast, especially after he'd seen Reg looking at her. He needed to mark her in some way, even if only to put his scent on her skin.

"Ooooh!"

Jessica squealed, but he was in heaven, pressing against her with his snout. She was his fated mate, after all. No one else could look or touch. Definitely no touching! Wait. His what?

Mate.

Claim.

Bite.

Mine.

Grrrr.

Chapter Twelve

"Oooh!"

Jessica groaned as something shoved her and she face planted on the carpet of the trunk of her little SUV.

What the heck?

One second, she was trying to grab Uncle Uzzi's packages with Reg chatting next to her, and the next something knocked her down. Something big and strong. But she wasn't afraid. Not exactly.

Gulp.

Heat pooled between her legs, and she had to clench them together to stave the flow as her inner Tiger purred away. The thing that knocked her down was sniffing about her bottom, paying atten-tion to the sliver of exposed skin under her butt cheek. Using her Shifter senses, she took a deep breath.

A Bear?

Shit.

Not just any Bear.

Her Bear.

Her inner she-Cat chuffed happily. It was definitely Brayden. But what the heck was he doing?

His warm breath tickled the flash of skin that peeped out through the rip in her jeans, and she couldn't help the shiver of arousal that ran through her. More liquid heat pooled between her legs, and she had to bite back her moan.

Dammit.

His animal would most certainly smell her arousal, and she had enough humiliation after he hadn't called her. It had been days since their date with no word or sign he wanted another, and Jess wasn't sure how she felt about that.

"Will you quit it?" she murmured.

Jessica tried pushing against him with her butt so she could get out of the damn car. But he didn't budge. Not one inch, the big bastard.

Ugh.

"Really? You know, personal space is a real thing," she grumbled and tried again.

The big Black Bear gently bumped her again with his long ursine snout, tickling her with his hot breath before stepping back. Finally, the dope was giving her space to stand.

She did so, slowly, turning around and meeting the jet-black eyes of Brayden's beautiful animal. He was large as a man, but as a Bear he was positively fucking monstrous. And so beautiful it almost hurt to look at him.

She sighed as she took in his handsome Bear. Jessica was not afraid. He didn't mean her any harm. Though his intentions were unclear, her she-Cat knew she was not in any kind of danger.

On the contrary, he seemed intent on helping her or something. Head cocked to the side the Bear watched her with glittering black eyes. His nose sniffed the air, lips opening and closing, tasting it in that cute way Bears had of scenting things.

Unable to help herself, Jessica reached out with her hands. She just had to touch him. Slowly at first, to see if it was okay. Shifters weren't pets, and not everyone was okay being handled.

But this Bear grunted happily and pushed his head further into her touch. Okay, so he liked to be petted. She smiled and ran her fingers over his face and neck, and up and down his back as far as she could reach.

"You're so warm and soft."

Jessica gasped and laughed as he snorted and sniffed her palm, breathing hot air into it till it tickled. She had expected his deep mahogany fur to be coarse and rough, but it was surprisingly thick and velvety. So smooth and warm to the touch.

Black bears in the wild were much like their Shifter cousins in that they came in many shades of color, despite their name. Black Bears could be brown, black, a combination of both, and some were even a light buff color near to white.

She sighed, heart doing double time, as Brayden sat on his back haunches and leaned into her. As if he was silently urging her to increase the pressure of her hands. She obliged him, loving the feel of the big Black Bear under her fingers.

She knew they were alone in front of the Pride House. Her Tiger could detect no other people or Shifters present. Strange, since there was always someone hanging around. Biting her lip, she stepped closer, drawn to the big animal and, if she were being honest, to the man within.

In just a few days, he'd become incredibly important to her. She'd been wondering about him.

Guessing what he was feeling and thinking for most of the time they'd been apart.

It was the way of Shifters, she supposed. This fast insta-lust and extreme attraction. She just didn't know her heart would be so involved. And it was. Big time.

His Bear hummed and purred, encouraging her to continue petting him. When she was as close to him as she could get, something completely unexpected happened.

One minute, she was running her hands over his furry head and neck, the next she was touching smooth, muscular skin.

Naked skin.

Jessica gasped and moved to step back, but Brayden held her close. His unrelenting grip on her hips meant she was trapped against him. She was strong as a She-Cat, but her strength was nothing compared to the raw power rolling off the Bear Shifter.

Brayden was just so much more dominant than she'd ever guessed. He could probably be an Alpha if he wanted.

Towering over her, his eyes darkened as he tightened his hold, tucking her carefully into his body as if she were fragile and small. She swallowed hard.

She was totally at his mercy like this. The question was, was Jessica a willing victim?

Yes.

Of course she was. She'd wanted this big, sexy man to hold her since she'd been awakened to the possibility that he was the man for her.

Gulp.

Heat filled her stomach in response to the deep growling coming from him.

No. Not a growl. That sound was more like a purr. Jessica was stunned. The big, naked--- *did she mention naked*, Bear was purring against her.

Strong, steely bands that were his arms wrapped tightly around her. The thick bar of his erection pressed against her belly. He was flustered, holding onto his control by a thread, and he was definitely aroused. And it was all because of her.

Jessica's panties practically melted off her body. She was so warm, so wet. She knew he could smell her desire, but that was alright with her. She could smell his, too.

It was almost too much to comprehend. The sexy Bear Shifter wanted her. Jessica moved against him, loving the groan that pulled from his throat. She felt powerful, feminine, her nerves buzzing with electricity and awareness.

Yes, please.

"Uh, Brayden?"

"You stopped," he murmured, dipping his head down to the hollow of her neck.

"I don't want you to stop, Jess. I like it when you touch me."

Jessica's mouth went dry at that confession. She had never really touched Brayden before. Truth be told, she liked it too. Liked the feel of the big hard Shifter under her hands.

Want more, the Tiger hissed.

He rumbled against her, pressing his mouth against her overheated skin. Brayden's nose and lips grazed the skin of her neck, followed by the slow drag of his fangs. Jessica whimpered at the contact. The promised intent almost too much for her she-Cat.

Hell.

It was enough to force her heat cycle, though she'd never experienced one yet. Fuck, it felt good to be this close to him.

Really good.

She tugged her hands free without moving out of his arms. Then she ran them over his arms and shoulders, all the way up to play with the hair at the base of his neck.

Brayden purred louder, and she sighed, holding him right where she wanted him. His lips and tongue felt great against the exposed skin of her neck. His naked body felt pretty damn good, too. Especially the way it was pressed up against hers.

She cursed the clothing she wore that separated them. And she wondered at her own bold thoughts as they held each other, petting, and nuzzling one another right outside the Pride House.

When did I become a slut?

The second that naked man wrapped you in his arms, her Tiger replied.

Jessica shivered, but she wasn't cold. She never really bothered with a coat. As a Shifter, she typically ran hotter than most. Her off the shoulder sweater meant Brayden had easy access to her neck and, well, other things. Like her breasts.

They swelled against his chest, nipples hardening into pebbles at the very thought of him touching her, exposing her, putting his mouth on her.

Yes, please.

"Brayden," she said his name, more moan than intended, but she supposed that was okay.

"You smell like gingerbread cookies, spicy and sweet. So fucking tempting, Jess, you're making me insane with wanting you," he murmured.

His tongue darted out of his mouth, and he tasted the skin just below her ear.

Shit.

Jessica's eyes closed against the light whispery touch. The promise of untold pleasures only he could bring teased her senses.

She shivered with delight. Sighing and moving her body every time his lips grazed her skin. He kept the pressure ever so light, almost as if he were afraid he'd break her if he pressed any harder.

His almost-kisses were a form of erotic torture, she decided. Heightening her already growing arousal and whetting her appetite for him in ways she had no idea how to handle. Her nails scratched his shoulders, not enough to break the skin, but enough to make him groan against her neck.

She felt so small up against the mountain of a man. Secretly loving the way he towered over her. He was practically bent in half as he trailed kisses along her clavicle. Jess bit her lip, silencing her whimpers as he dipped his head lower to graze the tops of her breasts.

Oh please, oh please, oh please.

Heat filled her lower belly, her sex dripped moisture, making her damp panties positively soaked. She couldn't go inside the Pride House. Not now.

"Been thinking about this for days, kitten. So sweet, so beautiful," he murmured, calling her a pet name for the first time ever as he kissed along the visible line of her cleavage.

"But you, you haven't called me since lunch the other day," she whispered, and some of her hurt seeped into her voice.

Dammit.

She squeezed her eyes tight and cursed herself for breaking the spell between them. It was time to put on her big girl panties and have a real talk with the man.

Gulp.

Chapter Thirteen

She felt a gentle hand on her chin, lifting her face. When she finally opened her eyes, it was to find his almost black ones staring into hers. She scented his regret in the air, and again, wanted to pinch herself for ruining the moment.

Nah. The hell with that. Jessica had to know what was going on before this went further. It was her heart on the line here, and maybe, if she was lucky, his too.

"I want to apologize for my behavior, Jessica. I can't give you any excuse or reason that would be good enough for why I behaved that way," Brayden explained.

She knew he was being sincere. Her she-Cat

could sense it in his mannerisms, in his eyes, and in the scent he carried.

"I know, I should probably stay away from you. You're the Neta's sister, and you are so much more than I could ever endeavor to deserve, but I don't know if I can."

"You don't know if you can what?"

"Stay away from you," he whispered, eyebrows furrowed as he cupped her face.

Brayden's handsome face turned down in a frown. His black eyes glittered, fraught with concern. Jessica instinctively ran her hands over his shoulders and neck, wanting to soothe him and bring him comfort.

Now, why on earth would she want to do that? This man had given her so many mixed signals she didn't know which way was up, but somehow, she could not help herself.

Mate.

Her Tiger pushed the thought into her brain and her chest tightened. It was true then, and time she acknowledged it.

As soon as the idea emerged, she felt it right down to her bones. This man, this gorgeous Bear, was her fated mate. Her destiny. No doubt about it.

All this time, he'd known it too. And he'd been

fighting it tooth and nail. Anger and disappointment threatened to overwhelm her, but she pushed it down, refusing to let it interfere with the joy that bubbled through her at knowing she had a mate.

"Kitten," he pressed his forehead against hers.

"I think you know what I am about to say. I can scent the subtle changes in you. You feel it too, don't you?"

"I think so," she whispered back.

It was useless for most normals to hide their emotions from Shifters since lies and other things had distinct scents. But for someone who was born and raised a Shifter, it was positively pointless.

Jessica knew better than to cover or hide the way she felt. She'd learned early that Shifters, especially her brother, were excellent at detecting people's feelings and discovering naughty little she-Cat's hidden mischief. Rather than risk getting caught in a lie, she'd developed a way of simply locking up her feelings.

It had been lonely for her as a child. Hunter did his best, but they were a decade apart in age and a world apart in responsibilities. He'd had an entire Pride to run. She didn't want to burden him. But a mate. That was different. They were supposed to help you through the good times and bad.

Would Brayden be willing to do that for her? Was he truly saying what she thought he was saying? There was only one way to find out.

Honesty.

She needed to lower her walls and allow him to feel her emotions. The truth would set her free, or it would fucking bury her. No games or hiding behind excuses. Jessica needed the truth.

Ready or not, here I come.

"What about you, Brayden? I heard a little about your past, but are you sure you are ready to move on?"

He stiffened against her, but he didn't let go. That was a good sign. Wasn't it?

"I know you have questions---"

"It's not about questions. You were mated before. You were hurt. I know this and my heart breaks for you, but I need to know if this is right for you. I deserve to know if you can be committed to me before we move forward," she said.

Her chest hurt as she said the words, but more for him than because of him. Rumor had it, he'd been mated before and lost her due to an accident. Now, she felt it in her heart that he was her fated mate. But Shifters could claim others if their fated ones did not turn up. Mates could be bonded through a bite, sex, scratches, and sacred vows. It was not the same, but it was still something.

Losing a mate was terrible. It was like losing a part of oneself. She did not wish that on anyone, let alone the man her heart yearned for. The thought of him being bonded to another caused her heart to ache.

Regardless of how unfair it was to him, she could not stop her sadness and hurt. Pushing past the disappointment of never being his first and only would be rough, but she could do it if he were truly committed to them.

"My past was, I mean, what I went through was not the same as us, Jess," he said and seemed like he wanted to say more.

Brayden struggled to find the words, and she tried to move back, but he tightened his hold. She sighed and allowed him to keep her in his arms. She could give them both that comfort until he was ready to talk.

Jessica waited and nodded patiently.

"When you're ready, Brayden. I won't push."

"No, you deserve to hear it from me, not the rumor mill. It is true, I have a past, but I have never had a mate before."

It was her turn to be confused. Hunter himself

had said he'd found the big Bear on Pride lands after he'd lost his mate. In danger of going rogue, he'd taken him in and adopted him into the Pride, for which Jessica would be forever grateful.

"Valeri was my best friend's mate. He died, and she looked at me for comfort. I never thought I would find my own mate, and it seemed the least I could do for him. He was like my brother," he explained.

"But I would never, I mean, I could never feel for her, the way I feel for you."

That last part was said in a deep, gravelly voice that sent shivers of need through her body. Okay, so it was complicated. Life often was.

Jessica would listen, but first they needed to be honest with each other. Licking her lips she went to speak, but he beat her to it.

"But I want you to understand, nothing else is as important as this, sweet kitten. You are my fated mate, and I have every intention of claiming you. If you want me to," Brayden stated, easing back to look in her eyes.

"And you're mine, as well," she returned.

Staking her claim out loud with words felt good. Empowering and freeing where she'd been all bottled up before.

She felt his body tense, as if he'd made up his mind about something. Waiting patiently was not exactly her strongest suit, but she would try for him.

"I want to tell you all of it. All of my past."

"Okay," she encouraged.

"Yes, what I told Hunter was true. I was engaged to a girl, but she was not *my girl*. Valerie was mated to my best friend from home, John. He was in the Army and had been sent to Iraq. It was supposed to be a quick and easy tour, but those things never are. He was killed there, and in our grief, Valerie and I turned to each other. She later came to me and told me she was pregnant."

"Oh," Jessica said, her heart hurting for the big man.

"I thought the baby was mine," he continued.

His voice hitched a little when he said baby. Jessica couldn't blame him. She wrapped her arms around him, silently willing him to take from her strength to continue the tale and he did. Amazingly enough, he did.

"So, I asked her to marry me. One morning, there was a nasty thunderstorm, and I had to go to work. We were barely talking at that point. Hadn't gone near each other again. Never, in fact, after that one night. She was depressed, and I was young. I didn't know what to do. That day, she drove into a telephone pole and died on impact."

"Oh no," Jessica swallowed.

"Later, I learned the baby was John's, not mine, and the cub had died inside of Valerie the day before she'd killed herself. Her grief over losing that one last connection with him had made her suicidal. I blamed myself for a long time, and I've been carrying that guilt around with me."

Sorrow at the tragic loss of his friend, and the poor Sow, whose mind had broken with her heart, filled Jessica. Those feelings were quickly followed by sadness for Brayden. He'd carried this burden for so long, thinking it was his fault when all along he'd done the best he could.

"Oh Brayden, I am so sorry."

"It's my fault, I should have helped her-"

"You did help her. There was nothing you could have done."

"I guess I know that now. I just felt like it was my fault for so long, it's hard to stop that line of thinking. I feel I failed John somehow. Valerie too."

"It was a terrible tragedy, and I am sorry you had to go through that," she replied and meant it.

Her heart hurt so much for the big man. He'd been young and in pain. His friend's mate had obviously felt the pain as well. She knew from the stories what happened to mates separated by death. One often followed the other. This was just a touch more tragic to her because Brayden had gotten involved.

"I will always be sorry for what happened to them, but it's what led me here. To Maverick Point. And to you."

Hope sprung up inside of Jessica. For a moment, she feared he was about to tell her goodbye, but not now. Not when his eyes glittered once more with heat and desire. She felt the subtle changes in his body as he pressed it against hers.

"So, you mean it then? About us being mates and wanting a future?"

"Yeah, I mean it."

Brayden grinned, and she felt heat pool in her belly, and the slow, drugging pull of desire began its pulsating thrum inside of her. He was willing to try for happiness, even after all his pain.

With her.

What could be sexier than that?

"I think it's about time I kissed you, kitten. Wouldn't you agree?"

His words slid over her like warm honey, bringing her arousal to peak.

Fuck. Yes.

Jessica wanted to kiss him. More than anything, and she was just about to tell him so. But before she found the words, his head was already lowered.

Slowly, oh so carefully, giving her ample time to back away should she so desire it, Brayden leaned close.

His clean rain scent enveloped her, and it filled her nostrils. Heat from his body warmed her despite the sudden chill in the air. Jessica shivered at the contact.

It was the anticipation rather than the cold that made her body tremble so. Want, need, lust filled her, and something else, too. Something too big to utter into the fragile night air. She was afraid if she did, it would disappear on the cold winter breeze.

"Wait," Jessica stopped him, ignoring the pang of hurt she felt coming from the big man.

"No, I mean, that's not why I said stop. I want you to kiss me. But, uh, I've built a lot of dreams and have a lot of expectations on kissing, and uh, if you're my mate, well, I don't want you to fuck it up," she whispered, and bit her lip.

"I understand," he replied and grinned wildly.

Then took her face in one big hand and tugged her close.

"Trust me, kitten, I know just how to kiss you," he growled.

And fuck, did he ever.

Jessica whimpered as his mouth closed over hers. His big, strong hands held onto her neck and face as he nibbled on her lips first. Licking the seam, then piercing her mouth with his long, talented tongue.

Bears really knew how to use their prehensile lips. At least, he sure as fuck did. The kiss they shared was beyond amazing. Brayden did things to her mouth she'd only ever read about.

He tasted of fresh rain showers and pure heat. Her Tiger growled in approval. The she-Cat urged her to get closer to their Black Bear.

To rub her scent on him.

To mark him.

Claim him.

Mine.

There was no question as far as her feline was concerned. The Bear belonged to Jessica. To both halves of her soul.

Me-ow!

Her Tiger sniffed at her response. But still, she was right on board with it if it meant sinking her fangs into the sexy Bear and claiming him once and for all.

Jessica melted into him. She wrapped her arms around Brayden's neck and pulled bringing him closer to the trunk of the car, closer to her. As if he'd read her mind, he lifted Jessica up onto the trunk like she weighed nothing at all.

Fuck, that was hot. She loved the easy display of strength. Her inner Tiger purred with the pleasure of it. Moisture dripped from her slit, and she groaned. She needed something, anything, to take the edge off.

She needed *him*.

Closer.

Now.

Right fucking now.

Jessica opened her jean-clad legs wide enough to let him in. She wrapped them around his waist, squeezing tight as he locked his massive arms around her.

Her big Bear seemed perfectly fine with this new position. More than fine if the rumble in his chest and the hardness pressing against her sex meant anything.

Brayden growled and groaned as he continued to devour her mouth. The gentle exploration of their first kiss quickly gave way to something more. Something deep and passionate that lit raging bonfires of arousal throughout Jessica's entire body.

His hands roamed her back, hips, and ass. She moaned, loving the feel of his calloused fingers as he lifted the hem of her sweater and lightly grazed her belly and, finally, her lace covered breast.

Both of them groaned as his fingers found her nipple. He toyed with the hardened nub, rubbing, and twirling it between his thumb and forefinger. And never once did he stop kissing her.

It was fucking amazing. So amazing, Jessica forgot where they were until they were so rudely reminded.

"What the ever-loving fuck is going on out here?!"

She couldn't fucking believe it. Jessica was pussy-blocked by her interfering as fuck brother.

She could have screamed the second she heard Hunter's massive roar from the front porch of the Pride House.

Shit.

She supposed it was her own damn fault, getting carried away out here where anyone could see them. But how was a girl supposed to claim her mate if she kept getting interrupted at every turn?

Brayden's whole body went stiff, and his black

eyes glittered with his Bear. Jessica watched him closely, searching for any hint as to what he was feeling. Frustration seemed to be the foremost, but beneath it was something else. Something her Tiger seemed happy with, but the woman could not name.

"Brayden, get your ass dressed and inside. The Council just called with an update on that matter they brought to us. Jessica, Uncle Uzzi wants to see you," Hunter growled the commands.

The fucker had interrupted what was sure to be the best damn experience of her life, and before she could respond, his almighty *Neta-ness* turned and went back inside the house.

Pussy-blocker!

Her she-Cat hissed.

"Jessica, I'm sorry," Brayden said, his eyes intent on hers, "but this is not over. Just delayed."

The worry and trepidation that had been gnawing at her gut eased with his words. His eyes grew warm, turning back to that mahogany color she loved so as the Bear inside of him receded, allowing the man to show. His intentions were right there in his gaze, visible for her to read like words on paper.

She wasn't sure what exactly was going on inside

his head, and that sort of scared her. But it was a good kind of scared.

Like being on a rollercoaster, slowly climbing up the first peak with every click of the chain, sending hearts pounding before the cars reached the top. The anticipation was key, but it was what came after the climb that made the trip worth repeating, that sudden plummet into a wild, breathtaking ride.

Jessica was inching closer to falling in love. The realization was daunting, but only for a moment. After all, the big Bear was worth it. She was ready for whatever happened next with Brayden.

Hell, it would already be happening, if only her stupid pussy-blocking brother hadn't messed everything up.

Grrr.

That was her frustration talking again. But she could hardly be blamed for it.

"Okay," she returned.

She took a breath, loving the scent of rain and clean earth that drifted into her nose.

Brayden.

It soothed her animal despite the fact that Jessica's insides were all upside down. And now she was sexually frustrated to top it all off.

"After the Neta is done talking, I'll come find you and we will discuss what comes next, alright?"

Unable to find the right words, she nodded. Brayden ran his large, callused hand over her cheek and dropped a kiss on her lips before turning to run around the side of the building. He was probably going to find some clothes, she figured.

Exhaling a deep breath, Jessica slipped down from the trunk and gathered Uncle Uzzi's packages.

Maybe the old Witch had some pointers about mating. Not that she and Brayden needed any.

Prrrrr.

Chapter Fourteen

Mine.

Mate.

Claim.

Now.

Fucking shit.

His Bear had been reduced to one word grunted commands. The animal pushed at his skin, demanding to be set free once more so they could find and claim their mate.

His Bear was furious with the Neta for interrupting what was surely to be the beginning of one off the fucking charts mating with his she-Cat. And she was his. There was no more questioning what his beast had always known.

Ignoring it was no longer an option. And fighting

it was no longer appealing. Not since he'd had the briefest of tastes of his ginger flavored, she-Cat. He couldn't wait to dip his tongue into her honey. Would it be spicy, sweet like the rest of her?

Fuck. Stop thinking of her honey.

But he couldn't stop. Not since he'd scented her sweet cream as it pooled between her thick thighs. Damn, now he had a boner, and it was impossible to hide in the light gray sweats he'd grabbed before heading to Hunter's office.

He stood outside the door for a beat, willing his beast to calm down before he had to face the Neta. Too late. The man had scented him, and he was beckoned by his Neta's roar.

"Get the fuck in here, Brayden," Hunter commanded.

Shit.

The last thing he wanted to do was piss off the one man who could stand in the way of his happiness. The Neta led the Maverick Pride with justice and a sense of caring that most leaders lacked. He was more than fair and stronger than any other Tiger in the Pride.

But we are not a Tiger, his Bear growled.

Some species were a little sensitive about the mixing of Shifter groups, but Brayden had given the man and the Maverick Pride his undying loyalty. He would continue to do so and to serve the Neta well. As long as he didn't try to stop Brayden from claiming his mate.

Roarrr.

Now that he'd sipped ambrosia from her sweet lips, Brayden would not let her go. He couldn't. She was his one true and fated mate. The only being in the entire universe who made his heart and soul complete. He would do anything for her. She was his world now.

The knowledge made him dizzy with expectant hope. She was so sweet, so beautiful, and so much more than a fucking Bear like him deserved. But he would endeavor to be worthy of her. He would give his life for her. The things he was willing to do just to see her smile were fucking shocking, but no, not really.

Mine, growled the Bear.

Yes.

First, attend the Neta. Second, seek out Jessica.

Grrr.

The Bear quieted, accepting his terms, and settling down before Brayden opened the door. Inside. Mikey, Reg, Pierce, Lance, and Hunter were all waiting on him.

These were Hunter's top men, after Brayden of course. They formed an elite unit in the Pride. The Neta's personal guard, positions of honor indeed. They were good men. Brayden knew them well as they also made up the crew, he led for the Pride's construction company, Maverick Development.

"Thanks for gracing us with your fucking presence," Hunter growled.

His words were sharp, but Brayden allowed them to roll off his shoulders. Nervous energy filled the room, and he knew it was the others reacting to their Neta. Hunter was pissed.

"Neta," Brayden greeted him.

He averted his gaze, baring his neck slightly to show Hunter the respect he deserved while acknowledging his position as the Pride leader and Alpha male in the room.

"I just received a phone call," Hunter began, allowing his razor-edged teal gaze to stop and land on each of the men in the room before he continued.

"The rumor the Council warned us about the streak is confirmed. These fuckers are encroaching on our area. They are too lost within their beasts to be reasoned with. We need to come up with a plan."

"A streak?" Brayden asked, vaguely familiar with the term but wanting clarification.

"Yes. This small crew is definitely a streak. And it gets worse," he went on.

"It seems our former Beta, that fucking piece of shit Blake, had tried to recruit some sympathetic rogue Tigers to his side. While they were not swayed to act when he was alive, they now feel his death was unjust. These young rogues have formed a *streak*."

"I am sorry, Neta, I have not heard that word," Brayden replied, hoping for clarification.

"Yes, Bears do not have them. You see, much like our wild cousins, a Tiger Shifter *streak* is a rogue group of males acting together to hunt and kill, or in this case, to attempt to do just that."

"This streak is making death threats?" Reg asked.

The younger man had gained some maturity after almost siding with Blake before the Neta had chosen his Nari and presented her to the Pride.

Reg had gained even more respect after taking every shit job the Pride could throw at him as his penance. He was then given the position as one of the Nari's personal guards, doing a hell of a job at it too.

The now deceased Blake had caused a lot of issues with his perversion of Pride laws. He'd tried to cause dissension amongst the ranks by claiming an unmated Neta was not in control of either his

Tiger or the Pride. His plan backfired when Hunter found his mate.

Of course, as Brayden looked at the slimmer man with his tawny hair carelessly pulled back in a low ponytail and his lowrider jeans clinging to his hips, he felt his Bear rise up. This was the fucker who had thought to compliment Brayden's mate, to seek out her company.

The Bear didn't like that. Not one bit. In his defense, Brayden had not even been aware of his own intentions to claim the sweet Jessica as his own.

But now that he was aware, his Bear was ready to end the first person who even thought about looking at her with anything other than distant respect.

Okay. So he was a jealous fuck. What could he say? He swung his head back towards Hunter, who looked at him with one black eyebrow raised.

Fuck.

He'd have some explaining to do after this meeting, he just knew it.

We will make a good mate for her, his Bear said.

The Neta will be proud to have us for his sister. We are strong, loyal, and trustworthy. We can protect, honor, and love-

Love?

No.

He stopped that thought dead in its tracks. He wanted Jessica more than anything in the whole world, but he wasn't ready to admit any more than that.

Not yet.

He'd only just come around to facing the fact that they were meant for one another. All those years he'd spent mourning John and condemning himself for his role in Valerie's suicide.

Shit.

That was a situation he did not want to be thinking about right now. Even though he felt better after discussing it with his mate. He knew now that there was nothing he could have done for Valerie. Her heart had died the moment John's baby's heart had stopped beating.

He tried to refocus on the present. The deep tones of his Neta's voice both soothed and interested his animal. Possession and protective instincts raced through him at the mention of danger. No one would hurt his mate. If they tried, it would be the last thing they ever did.

Grrr, his Bear agreed.

"We will not allow anyone to harm the Pride, much less a bunch of misled cubs. This streak will be stopped. Reg and Pierce, I want you two in charge of upping our security measures. Lance, I want you to talk to the Pride. Go house to house if you must, but make sure everyone knows we are here, and we are watching. Mikey, I want you to make sure we have plenty of medical supplies should there be a fight," he said, issuing commands like the born leader he was.

Hunter's anger rose and the Shifters in the room could not help but react to it. Heads bowed, and jaws clenched. Brayden's body tensed, his animal on edge with the need to shift under his Neta's rage.

"Brayden, you are my Beta and head of my security team, you will set up sentries around town. I want Maverick Point protected."

"Yes, Neta," Brayden answered.

He noted more shuffling of feet, the baring of necks, and the low rumble of growls filling the air. But he remained still. There was something Hunter wasn't saying.

"Neta? Excuse me, but what else did the Council say?"

His Neta exhaled deeply. Whatever it was, the news was troubling his leader and Brayden braced himself. He was the Beta of the Pride. It was his job to support his leader in every way he could.

"Everyone is dismissed except for you, Brayden," Hunter said.

His face was impassive. His expression that of a leader and Brayden had nothing but respect for the man.

"What happened outside? I thought you were not taking a mate."

"Neta?"

Brayden was not sure if he wanted to just come out and tell his leader that he had been seconds away from claiming his mate. Or that he had every intention of fucking and biting his sister the second this meeting was over. Neither was probably wise at the moment.

"You and Jessica. What is that all about?"

"With all due respect, I think I should discuss things with Jessica before I speak to you," Brayden carefully lowered his gaze.

He had no wish to challenge the Neta, but some shit was private.

"Brayden, you are the best man I know, but I don't want to see Jessica used or hurt in any way. She's my sister," he emphasized.

"And she is my mate. I'll kill the man who says I am using her," he growled, raising black eyes to his Neta for one brief moment.

Brayden's voice had grown deep and thick with his Bear. The beast did not like Hunter's insinuation. How could he think Brayden would use a woman? Especially his sister.

Fuck.

The answer hit him hard.

The streak.

That rogue group of assholes must be starting some shit about his being a Bear in a Tiger Pride. Hunter snarled and stood up. He was angry, but even Brayden could see it wasn't with him.

"Is she really your fated mate?" the man asked.

"Yes, she is. I will not let anything happen to her, Hunter. Not while there is breath in my body."

Hunter's teal eyes glowed for a split second before a huge, shit-eating grin broke out along the bald man's face.

"You and Jess, huh?"

"Yes," Brayden repeated, and slowly, his face mirrored Hunter's grin.

"Have you claimed her yet?"

Hunter asked, all serious once more.

"No, uh, in fact, you interrupted our first kiss."

Brayden felt his face burn with the admission.

"Really? Shit bro, my bad," Hunter replied and shrugged.

"Okay, listen, this streak is claiming I have polluted our Pride by allowing a Bear to become my Beta. One of theirs has apparently been sending direct messages to one of the Council."

"What does that mean?" Brayden asked, heart pounding furiously.

The Bear wanted to protect what was his, that meant defending his position and his woman. And not in that order.

"It means nothing," Hunter growled.

"I am the Neta of the Maverick Pride, and no little shit is going to tell me who I can choose as my Beta."

Brayden smirked, relief flowing through his veins. He hated to admit he'd been scared for even a moment. But whatever else happened, he was still Pride Beta. and Hunter had his back.

"What does the Council want us to do?"

"Fuck the Council. They don't run this Pride either. I do," growled Hunter.

His voice heavily laced with his animal, he tapped his hand on his desk.

"I will deal with them. You go find your mate."

Brayden's eyes flashed. His Bear pushed against him, but he remained in control. Nodding to Hunter before he turned around to leave.

Whatever problems the rogue Tiger streak was causing could be dealt with later. His Bear grunted and rumbled deep in his chest. Muscles bunched, stomach tense, he made his way out into the Pride House. No more delays or misunderstandings.

Brayden had a mate to claim.

Chapter Fifteen

"You mean to tell me your pussy-blocking brother is still at it?" Uzzi Stregovich's expression went from amused to exasperated in under a second.

"I know, right?" Jessica rolled her eyes.

"Pussy-blocking?"

Elissa smirked. The Nari dissolved into a fit of giggles at the description of her mate as both Uncle Uzzi and Jessica looked on.

"Yeah, that big pussycat mate of yours does his best to ruin Jessica's fun times. He is a pussycat, and he is always blocking, pussy-blocker, yes? Hasn't Jessica told you?"

Uncle Uzzi stirred his tea, nodding at the two

young women and seemingly content in his butchering of modern euphemisms.

"No, uh, she hasn't," Elissa said, wiping her eyes.

"However, I'm more concerned with why you didn't bring me any of those sexy panty sets Uncle Uzzi told me about, Jess?"

Elissa growled at Jessica and looked through Uncle Uzzi's stack of cards and flyers promoting the new *Kisses By Kylie* winter sets.

"Lissa, I love you, but *ew*. Seriously, if you want some slutty underwear to wear for my brother, you will have to just come to the shop yourself."

Both Uncle Uzzi and Elissa laughed at Jessica's faux shudder. She'd been surprised to see them both sitting together when she thought Uncle Uzzi's schedule was full, but this emergency meeting of her brother's meant the women had a chance to catch up.

"So, how are you feeling, dear?" Uncle addressed his question to Elissa.

"Fine. This little cub of mine is growing every day and I have never been so happy. Thank you so much, Uncle Uzzi!"

"Oh, it's my pleasure, really. And the cooking?"

"Oh, my gods! So, these Tigers really love to eat,

and I get to try out new recipes all the time. I have never been so happy," she answered.

"I can see that. These butter cookies are to die for. I must have the recipe. And now, Jessica, why don't you tell us what is going on with this Bear of yours? Have you decided to take him by the horn yet?"

Uncle Uzzi wiggled his eyebrows, and Elissa busted out laughing once more. The old Witch rose from his chair to get more hot water for the teapot, and Jessica shook her head at her Nari. She was incorrigible lately. But that's what happened with the sudden appearance of a sex life, she supposed.

"OMG! Yes, Jess, please I need the deets," Elissa said, mimicking holding on to another type of horn behind Uzzi's back.

Jessica felt her cheeks heat and knew she must be the same shade as an overripe tomato. She squirmed in her seat under Uncle Uzzi's and Elissa's watchful stares.

"Well, um, we um sort of, almost well, I just don't exactly," she shrugged.

"What do you mean you don't know?" Elissa asked.

"I believe she means they have not had sex, correct?" Uncle Uzzi asked with his usual frankness.

Jessica's face burned even hotter. She shook her head, refusing to look at either of them.

"You must not be embarrassed. I am a Witch and Elissa here is a Tiger now. Sex is perfectly natural and necessary for a true mating," he added.

Still, she refused to talk. It was beyond embarrassing. How was she going to explain that Brayden had taken her to lunch, disappeared for two days, then kissed the hell out of her in front of the whole dang Pride House. Where was there time for sex?

It had been lunch, followed by two days of nothing, then he had his big old Bear snout up her behind all of twenty minutes ago. That was followed by his very human tongue ramming down her throat.

They'd admitted they were mates to each other, but then big bro had interrupted. Brayden had said they weren't finished, but that was not exactly a statement that he was going to claim her.

Fucking hell.

Jessica shook her head. She was confused and frustrated.

"We haven't had sex. This was only the first time he kissed me, so as for this Tiger taking any Bear by the horn, it just hasn't happened."

"Really? Hell, Hunter had me naked and bent

over within minutes of meeting me," Elissa said, then blushed furiously.

"We know, dear."

Uncle Uzzi smirked and winked at the pregnant female. Jessica felt a zap of jealousy, quickly followed by a doozy of insecurity. She hated that, but it was hard not to feel kind of rejected.

"Brayden is a tough nut to crack, Jessica. I'm sure it won't be long until he has you screaming his name," Uzzi said gently.

"Uncle Uzzi, I don't know whether to be horrified or comforted by your words," Jessica responded, covering her face with her hands.

"You know what," Elissa piped in.

"I read in this romance book that Bear Shifters, especially drop-dead gorgeous ones like our hunky Beta, are known for giving some of the best damn oral this side of the universe. So the question is, besides that overprotective mate of mine, how do we get Brayden to jump your bones?"

"OMG! Lissa, not in front of Uncle Uzzi," she whispered.

"Dears, I know this will come as a shock, but I know all about sex. DO not forget my clients are almost ninety-five percent Shifters. Please, you can discuss anything with me. I swear it does not leave these lips."

"Thank you, and of course, I didn't mean to say I did not trust you---"

"That is perfectly fine my dear."

"The truth is, well, I think I must be lousy at sex," Jessica confessed.

"Nonsense!"

"Oh honey, why?" Elissa asked, brows furrowed.

"I don't exactly inspire great passion in men. I never have any way. What if I don't turn him on?"

"Jessica, you need to start thinking positive. You are beautiful and just as sweet as honey. If you are mates, you turn him on, alright. You just need time alone together. Hmm," Uncle Uzzi said.

He tapped the table with his blunt fingernails, the sound loud in the suddenly quiet room.

"I don't know. What if he doesn't want me like that? He was engaged before, the situation was complicated, but it ripped his heart out. Maybe he doesn't have anything left to give," Jessica's voice hitched at the end.

That possibility terrified her more than anything else. Her inner feline chuffed and shook her head. Her beast refusing to allow doubt to creep its way inside of her brain. Not now when everything she had ever wanted was so close.

"Look, I think you will get to the physical aspect of mating soon enough. It is your heart you must consider carefully," Uzzi replied.

Jessica nodded. She had no doubt he was right. After all, Brayden was a Shifter, and the mating fever would hit him, eventually.

But what about love? There were some things having sex, even great sex, would never fix. Jessica wanted to climb the mountain of a man and experience the kind of intimacy she had only ever dreamed about. But deep down in the secret, or not so secret, recesses of her mind, Jessica hoped for love as well.

"I agree with you, Uncle Uzzi. Sex is fine, and it is important, don't get me wrong, Jessica. But tell me something, you keep talking about how *he* feels. What about you?" Elissa asked.

"Yes. That is a good question, Elissa. Jessica, do you know how you feel about the Bear?"

Uncle Uzzi leaned forward.

"What do you mean?" Jessica hedged.

"You said the Neta interrupted your first kiss. Well. How was it?" Uncle Uzzi asked.

"The kiss?"

"Yes. When you spoke to me the other day, you

told me a lot about what you have spent hours imagining your mate's kisses and what they would be like. You've kissed the Bear. So, what was it like?"

Warmth flared inside her, spreading from her core and through her belly, racing inside her veins till it reached all her limbs. Of course, she remembered the heated kiss she and Brayden had shared. It was only a short while ago.

"It was, um, it was nice," she said, settling for something bland.

"Nice?" Elissa spat the word out, as if Jessica had said it was gross or something.

"Yes," she repeated.

"It was *nice*."

For some reason she did not want to reveal just how deeply his kiss had affected her. Nice did not begin to cover it, but it was so new, so raw. How could she share it yet? Even with two of her most trusted friends.

No, she had not known either for very long, but she had immediately categorized them both as trustworthy. Jessica cared very much for the old Witch and her new sister-in-law. But was this something she should talk about so soon?

"Oh dear, you can do better than that, can't you?"

Uncle Uzzi's mischievous smile should have

tipped Jessica off, but her Tiger remained at ease. Then she realized he was not looking at her. Tingles of awareness rippled down her spine and she tensed.

"Yes," a deep voice spoke up from behind her.

"We can do better than nice."

She gasped, startled into whipping around so fast she almost fell off her chair. Even Shifter Cats could be clumsy, and she would have fallen too, if not for the pair of enormous, strong arms that wrapped around her. The owner of that voice pulled her to her feet and dragged her closer until she was flush against his hard, hot body.

"*I* can do better," Brayden whispered, and his words drew a whimper of need from her open lips.

Black eyes glittered down at her and his chiseled face was further defined by the short-cropped beard he wore. It seemed longer than it had been that morning, signs his Bear was present.

The color of his hair was lighter than his Bear. The brown was streaked in front with sun-kissed golden waves probably from his time outside during work. The beard was darker still, but Jess didn't mind. She liked facial hair on a man. No, not just any man.

Her man.

The temperature inside the room rose a few notches, and she felt as if everything else faded away under his stare. Brown eyes bled to black, and Jess licked her lips hungrily. She loved his Bear was so close, and that she was the one to push him that way. It made her feel desirable, powerful, and just a little bit sexy.

"You are all those things, kitten," he whispered so lowly only she could have heard him.

"Okay, well, if you would excuse us. Come Elissa," Uncle Uzzi said.

"We'll just, um, be going," Elissa replied, taking Uzzi's outstretched hand.

The Nari needed a little help rising to her feet. Her pregnant belly protruded in front of her, and she laid one hand on the babe that grew inside her womb. Giggling, she hurried out of the room with Uncle Uzzi. Undoubtedly to find her own mate.

"You smell good," Brayden said, capturing her attention.

Time stood still as he rubbed his nose over the exposed skin of her right shoulder. She was gonna feature that fucking sweater on her website under the section *things to wear to drive your man gaga.*

Seriously, he did not seem able to stop himself from nuzzling her skin, and Jessica loved it. The feel of his warm breath as he just breathed in her scent made her shiver with desire.

As if he knew just what it did to her inside, Brayden repeated the gesture. But this time, he added his lips, tongue, and teeth to the mix. If she wasn't desperate for him before, she was getting there now. And in a hurry.

"Don't stop doing that," she moaned as his pliable lips latched onto her earlobe.

His Bear growled while he nibbled. Big, rough hands ran up and down her body, sending little sparks of desire throughout. He was wearing sweats now, and a shirt, the casual attire Hunter kept stocked around the Pride House for anyone needing a quick change.

Shifters did not typically care about nudity, but ever since Hunter had mated Elissa, he'd been pretty easily riled by naked men strutting around his mate. Jessica did not mind the material, but she wanted to feel all of him, hot and hard against her skin.

Brayden growled and her body responded. Heat pooled between her thighs and her nipples hardened into tiny pebbles. She ached, actually fucking ached as he ran his amazing hands up and down her back, over her wide, round hips, until he was firmly cupping her ass.

His nimble fingers found the tear in her jeans and Brayden's growl grew louder. He teased her skin, sliding his hand inside the material to knead her plump flesh. Her breath hitched as his fingertips teased the patch of lace that covered her cheeks.

"These fucking jeans are making me crazy," he groaned and flexed his hips, pressing the steel rod of his cock against her belly.

"Yeah?"

"Most definitely," he said, teasing her lips with his own.

Never quite meeting, just soft brushes of his impossibly nubile lips over hers, like short glimpses of the kiss they shared. Jessica wondered if a person could die from longing.

Brayden's delicious mouth hovered close, so close to her own. His breath tickled, mingling with hers as he left whisper soft touches on her mouth and cheeks, even her nose.

"Brayden," she moaned his name.

The moisture between her thighs increased. Her stomach contracted. She desperately wanted him to close those few millimeters between them. To feel his soft, warm mouth against hers.

"What is it you want sweet Jessica? Tell me."

"Your mouth," she demanded.

"Gods, I want your mouth. *Please.*"

"That's all you had to say," he replied and smirked.

She could've kicked him. She would too. Later. After he finished kissing the fuck out of her mouth.

Prrrrrr.

Chapter Sixteen

rayden's Bear had already picked up the scent of his luscious mate in the air when he exited the Neta's office.

Sure, the briefing had been troublesome, but it fell from his mind the second he got a trace of honey, nutmeg, and ginger in his nostrils. She was still there, inside the Pride House.

Relief and urgency rushed through his blood at the thought of Jessica so close. She hadn't left yet, and he could still catch up to her. Maybe even finish what they'd started outside.

Find. Kiss. Claim.

His Bear roared the words in his mind's eye. And yes, the notion held merit. Brayden was big enough to admit he was done pretending he could live without her. At least, he could admit that much to himself.

His Bear pushed him to move faster. Particularly when he thought of the other single, unmated males that lurked nearby. If any of them went near his unclaimed mate made, his beast was going to go wild. He looked down to see claws tipping his hands and fur sprouting along his arms.

Fuck.

He had to get a grip on his Bear before he sought her out. As if sensing his plans, the Bear receded, allowing Brayden's human self to act once more in control.

Even his animal understood there were things only the human side of him could accomplish. Such as claiming their sexy as hell mate. Hunting her scent through the house had him even more on edge.

He finally found her sitting in the informal dining room with Elissa and Uncle Uzzi. Brayden had had his doubts about the Witch, but now he realized he owed his future happiness to the powerful man.

Without him, he would have never had the courage to go beyond his own past to acknowledge the female the Fates had sent him.

His sweet Jessica.

Beautiful.

Mine.

He felt his chest rumble with his Bear. The animal purring in approval, anxious to be near his mate. His ears picked up on the conversation the three of them were having, and quickly, his ears turn red. They were discussing his and Jessica's as of yet, non-existent sex life.

Fuck that.

He would make sure his sexy little She-Cat would have something else to blush about the next time she was asked about his prowess.

Hell fucking yes.

The second he tugged her into his arms, the others in the room simply ceased to exist. His hands trembled when he got them on her, but only at first. After that, he knew exactly how to tease and touch his sexy little she-Cat.

His Bear pushed to take over, but he was in control now. It took a lot of strength to rein the animal in, kissing Jessica, taking more of his atten-tion than he ever could have imagined. She was more intoxicating than anything he'd ever expe-rienced.

He was vaguely aware of the sounds of footsteps coming down the hallway. Without thinking, he swept Jessica off her feet into his arms. Swallowing her startled moan. He continued to kiss her as he made his way hurriedly to his suite of rooms.

Luckily, as Beta, Brayden had been given his own wing inside the Maverick Pride House. It was necessary for him to be close to the Neta and to the Nari. But because of the previous tenant, he'd gutted the place.

As soon as Blake had been disposed of, Brayden had torn down walls, replaced sheetrock, and flooring. He'd repainted, re-tiled, and replaced every single inch of furniture. He'd wanted nothing of the man's evil left to taint the space.

Now that he'd brought his mate here, he was glad he'd gone through all the trouble. Not only was this place new and clean, but he'd also reinforced the insulation in the walls to make it soundproof. The perfect den for a Bear and his mate.

Mine.

He eased the door closed and clicked the lock in place. Jessica smiled against his lips, her tongue exploring the inside of his mouth.

Fuck, she was so damn sexy. Thank the gods she was his.

Brayden wasn't into sharing. He might have been a complete ass for not calling her for two days, but he'd make it up to her no matter how long it took. As a matter of fact, he was going to start right now.

"Brayden," Jessica sighed his name as he sat her down on the bed.

Before she could say another word, he reached for the end of her sweater and tugged the soft fabric over her head. He needed her naked. The sooner the better.

Grrrrr.

The sight before him made his cock throb mercilessly. Little pieces of silvery lace barely covered her plentiful breasts, making his mouth water. She tried to cover her belly with her arms, but he would have none of that. He wanted to see every inch of her pale ivory skin.

"So beautiful," he breathed, taking her hands away from her stomach and placing them next to her.

"I'm too big," she murmured.

"You. Are. Fucking. Perfect." His growl reverberated in the room.

"I'm a Bear, kitten, and you fill my hands like you were made for me."

"Oh yeah?"

"Fuck yeah. Your skin is like fresh peaches and

cream," he growled, his voice was thick with his Bear.

"Your scent is like honey and gingerbread. And your taste, sweeter than all of those combined. Need you, mate."

The heady scent of her arousal filled the room, making his animal rumble. He liked that she was turned on by him. It was natural for mates to want each other, but nothing in this world was a certainty. He'd learned that the hard way when his friend had died.

Not now, he pushed the thought out of his head.

He'd loved John like a brother and mourned Valerie's death, even going so far as to take on the guilt for it, but not now and not here.

Here was for his mate.

Jessica. Kitten. Mine.

"Your turn," she whispered boldly.

Brayden's nostril flared and his dark eyes widened as she brought her hands down to the button of her jeans, tapping the little piece of copper as she waited for him to do something.

Wait.

What did she say?

Fuck.

His brain had turned to mush. Rushing like a

madman, he tore his t-shirt off of his body and took his sweatpants off in one hard shove.

"You're behind now, baby," he said, grinning when she couldn't take her eyes off his cock.

"Holy fuck," she whispered.

"Bear Shifter, kitten. I'm big all over."

And he was. Tall and covered in sinewy muscle. He had big hands, big feet, and yes, everything else in between was big, too. Grabbing his dick with his right hand, he stroked himself from root to tip, liking the way Jessica's eyes followed the movement. The unique teal color glowed with her Tiger.

So, the she-Cat was interested in what he had to offer, eh? He groaned and spread the pearl of precum over his mushroomed head, cupping his balls with his other hand and giving in to the pleasure of touching himself while his mate watched.

"No, let me," she said, falling to her knees in front of him.

Brayden was so stunned he couldn't move. Nothing could have gotten him prepared for the sight of his gorgeous woman on her knees.

Holy fucking hell.

His sexy mate leaned forward and kissed the tip of his cock with her full pink lips. Then her tongue snaked out, licking the next bead of precum that oozed from his dick.

"Fuck," he groaned.

She replaced his hand with her own. Her sigh rivaling his as she took his long cock down her throat and sucked. The sounds of her licking and swallowing him were so fucking sexy his cock grew even harder.

"Fuck, kitten, you look so fucking good with your lips wrapped around my dick," he growled.

"That's fucking beautiful, baby. Suck me, yeah, just like that," Brayden growled.

He threw his head back and allowed himself to get lost in the pleasure of his mate's ministrations. She was so fucking good at giving him what he wanted, what he needed, when he didn't even know himself.

Her claw-tipped fingers grasped his hips, the points biting into his skin. They added just a hint of pain to the unbelievable pleasure she was giving him making it that much more intense.

"Fuck, kitten, I'm gonna come if you don't stop,"

he warned, but Jessica didn't seem to have any intentions of stopping.

Her fingers dug into his flesh, and she deep-throated him, sucking his dick with gusto.

"Fuck, gods, yes," he groaned, long and hard as he came inside her hot mouth.

Did she squirm or move away?

Nope.

His Jessica swallowed every fucking drop, and if he didn't love her before, he sure as fuck did right then.

"Mmm," she moaned, sitting back on her heels and grinning like the she-Cat she was.

"Kitten, that was so fucking hot," he growled, more Bear than man.

Brayden pulled her to her feet and crashed his mouth into hers. He tasted himself on her lips, and fuck if that didn't turn him on. He fucking loved that she was covered in his scent. The Bear wanted to give her more.

More of his cum. More of his dick. More of him.

Claim.

Bite.

Mine.

Grrr.

"My turn," Brayden growled, grabbing her jeans.

He almost tore them off before he remembered he liked this particular pair. Jessica sucked in long, deep breaths as Brayden laid her down, and deftly relieved her of every article of clothing she had on.

Her bright teal eyes watched his every move. Making him aware that he was mating a Shifter whose grace and power were a thing of fucking beauty to be treated with respect and care.

And he would. Forevermore.

With every inch of skin he revealed, he stopped what he was doing to properly touch and kiss. He whispered words as he went from place to place. Naughty, secret words, praising his mate for her beauty and strength.

"Touching you is the most incredible kind of high," he said, nipping the skin over her hip with his teeth.

She had gorgeous hips. Round and luscious, perfect for holding on to while he pounded into her. But he had other things to do first.

"Brayden, please," she begged, thrusting her hips in silent invitation.

His chest rumbled and saliva filled his mouth. He knew what his mate wanted, and he was more than ready to give it to her. But first, he needed a taste.

"You know, Bears love honey, kitten. I think I

need some of yours before I fill you with my cock," he rumbled as he lowered himself onto the bed.

Brayden sucked in a deep breath, savoring the spicy sweet scent of her desire as he came face to face with heaven. Licking his lips, he leaned forward and snaked out his tongue to swipe at her dripping pussy. So pretty and pink, she was glistening with her arousal in the dim light of the bedroom.

"Mmm," he groaned as her spicy flavor burst on his tongue.

She was sweeter than his very best favorite kind of cookie. All that gingerbread intensity and honey sweet icing. Her natural nutmeg and ginger flavor mixed with the heady musk of her desire had his Bear roaring at him to stake his claim.

"Oh gods," she mewled, bucking her hips in time with his own ministrations.

Passion flared and Brayden grabbed her hips, holding her captive to his sensual tortures. He drove his tongue into her heat, fucking her on the appendage the way he would with his cock.

Soon.

Very soon.

"Need you, Brayden," his mate moaned as her pussy squeezed his tongue.

Her orgasm so close now. He added one finger to

her heat and set his tongue to flicking the hard bundle of nerves hidden beneath her soft red curls.

"Taste so good, kitten. I can't get enough of you," Brayden groaned.

"Need you, mate," she moaned, thrusting harder against his mouth.

"Gonna fuck you. Gonna claim you. But you have to come on my tongue first."

"I don't think I can," she gasped, and leaned up on her elbows.

She looked stunning. Her round breasts heaving, the pink tips puckered and hard. Those crazy, beautiful teal eyes of hers were glittering at him, and her mouth was open invitingly as she moaned and gasped. Brayden held her gaze and continued to fuck her with his tongue and hands.

It was the most erotic thing he'd ever done, sucking on her pussy while she watched. It gave him an incentive to work harder than he ever had. And he did, giving her everything he had inside him.

It was hers. Always had been. Always would be.

"Oh gods, close," she moaned, keeping her eyes on him.

Brayden's gums ached, his fangs lengthening, and he did something he'd never done before. He kept pumping two fingers in and out of her sex, and another circled her dark forbidden hole. Flicking the flat of his tongue along her clit, he held her eyes in his, and then he scraped his fang along the little nub. Then, and only then, did his woman shatter.

Fuck yeah.

His Bear roared while she came apart in his arms. She roared his name, loud and long as she came and came.

Still licking her, Brayden swallowed down every drop of her cream like she was his own personal slice of heaven.

And she was.

Mine.

Chapter Seventeen

The man has fucking wrecked me.

She tried catching her breath. But who needed air? She gasped and moaned. Breathing was completely overrated, wasn't it? Especially when her *soon to be claimed mate* was using his long tongue and prehensile lips to make her orgasm like a fucking rock star.

Holy fuck, the man had skills. And Jessica was one lucky pussycat. She pulled on Brayden's hair, loving the feel of her big Bear as he slid up her body.

He was all hard planes and rippling muscles. Heat from his skin seared hers, marking her with his scent. His chest rumbled and waves of desire filled her.

"You feel so fucking good," he growled, hands cupping her large breasts.

She'd never been so happy to be plus sized in her whole life, but he was right. Her lush softness was the perfect contrast to his hard muscles. She could not wait to get to the part where her possessive Bear worshipped her plump body, as long as he knew that was not all Jess was.

She might be fluffy, but she was also a Tiger. A motherfucking badass who was strong and fierce. She could more than take the weight of his heavy body, and even as he tried to hold himself away, she wrapped her legs around his waist and pulled him down on top of her.

"I'm too heavy," he grumbled.

"You're perfect for me, mate," she growled back and nipped his lip between her teeth.

Truth was, Jessica loved every ounce of the beast and man who belonged to her. Fated mates were designed to bring completion to their other halves, and he was hers in every way. She wanted to feel the pressure of his body, the penetration, the dominance.

With a mighty growl and his black eyes glittering down at her, Brayden caught her lips. Another soul searing kiss and she never wanted to be completely possessed by another soul until that moment. As if he'd read her mind, Brayden's thick cock was suddenly at her aching core, nudging her wet nether lips to allow him entry.

She spread her legs wide. Opening for him, surrendering to him, and loving every second of it. Jessica lifted her hips, wrapping her long legs around his waist, urging him to sink deep, hard and fast. But the bastard made her wait, too strong and steady to be rushed, much to her consternation.

"So tight," he moaned as he proceeded to invade her body one inch at a time.

Did she mention it was a whole lot of inches, too? Like a lot. By the time he was halfway seated inside her tight and untried channel, Jessica felt impossibly full. And so fucking good. All her synapses were firing, nerve endings on high alert, and she was desperate for him to move.

Thank you, universe.

She gasped as he stretched her sheath to the max with his impossibly enormous cock. After waiting a moment for her to adjust, he finally slid all the way home, drawing matching groans from them both.

"Fuck, kitten, you feel so good squeezing my cock with that pretty little pussy," he growled, kissing her on the mouth.

Not a tiny little kiss, either. This was a full on assault. Brayden destroyed her with that kiss, plundering her mouth and moving his tongue in time with his cock.

"My pussy's not pretty," Jessica responded the moment he let her breathe again.

Possessive bastard. But he was sexy and hung. Thank fuck. She was barely able to form a coherent thought with him so deep inside her sheath.

"The fuck you say, kitten? My pussy is fucking gorgeous," Brayden grunted as he withdrew, causing her to whimper.

The arrogant prick grinned at her mewling noises. He held himself up, waiting for her eyes to focus back on his.

"Say it, kitten. Tell me how pretty my pussy is," he demanded, withholding his cock until she complied.

Motherfucker. She was gonna get him back for this. Later. After he made her come a time or twelve.

"Brayden, please," she hissed.

He slid in a few inches, then pulled out once more, causing the flames of arousal to burn a little higher with each teasing slide.

"Say it," he demanded again.

"Fine, but if you don't make me come soon, I'm gonna scratch the hide off you," she snarled.

He grinned, eyes glittering, as he swiveled his hips, causing the thick knob of his mushroomed head to brush against her swollen and needy clit. Fucking hell. Jessica wanted to scream. So she did.

"My pussy is pretty."

"MY pussy," he corrected.

"Yes. Yours! Your pussy is motherfucking gorgeous!"

"Mine," he snarled, then pounded into her in one long, hard thrust.

"Yes!" she screamed.

Her she-Cat had her claws coming out, fangs too, in reaction to the possessive growl coming from his chest. She was more than happy to see his beast come out to play. It meant both man and animal were united in this. In his claiming of her. And she sure as hell hoped he intended to claim her fully and completely.

That was all the time she had for thought. Brayden was doing things to her she'd only ever read about. Lost in sensation, Jessica let go for the first time in her adult life. She wanted to drown in him, in the delicious naughty things he was doing to her.

His magnificent dick seemed to light fires in every single one of her nerve cells. So incredibly thick, his pulsing member slid in and out of her channel with precise, powerful thrusts. Like he was trying to touch every centimeter of her body, and the man was, too.

"Mine," he growled the word.

Jessica nodded. It was the only response she could give. She was his, and he was hers. Together, they were better and stronger. A mated pair who would only know full, complete happiness in each other's arms. It was a miracle, and she was going to hold on to it, *to him*, with both hands.

It might be too soon to confess how deeply she loved him, but maybe not. They were Shifters, not normals. Fated mates did not always love instantly, but she'd known Brayden for years. He was a good man, an excellent Beta, and as a mate, he was already knocking her socks off. Brayden worked her body, playing it like a master played his instrument, hitting every spot just right.

Thrust, withdraw, swivel, and thrust again.

Each move had her gripping him tighter with her legs and arms. She clutched at his shoulder, enjoying his hiss when her nails scratched him, marking him in her own way.

He dipped his head, swallowing her moans with his mouth, mashing his lips to hers. Each kiss was filled with such heat and intensity, her belly tight-ened, and toes curled.

Warm, drugging sensations of pure bliss began to swirl, starting in her core. That build up teased and excited her with hints of promised fulfillment and ecstasy.

Need. Want. Claim.

"Want you so bad, Jessica, always. Want you to be mine. Say you are mine," he growled, the words so deep she almost couldn't hear.

"Yes," she answered, knowing it was the only possible thing she could say.

"Mine!" he demanded.

"Yours," she responded.

Her she-Cat purred, loving his possessive streak. Brayden increased the speed and pressure of his thrusts, bringing them all the way up the bed, till they were at the headboard. When they could go no farther, he took them both right off the mattress, onto the floor. Careful of her head, he caught their fall with his arms, grabbing a pillow as he continued to slam into her pussy. Jessica did not care as long as he never stopped. Her impending orgasm grew with every withdraw and pump of his hard body until she was lost to everything but the sensation of it, of him.

"Can't stop, kitten. Won't stop until I fill you with my cum, mark you with my bite," he growled again.

Jessica noted the glittering of his eyes, like black diamonds in the dark room. The hint of fangs in his mouth had her own gums aching. Anticipation thrummed up her spine. Her Bear's growling as he fucked her senseless made it that much more intense.

It was what she wanted, what she needed. So damn good. He was so thick and hard, her pussy spasmed around his cock. Jessica knew without a doubt she was giving him more than her body. This claiming was about body, mind, heart, and soul.

After searching for her mate for most of her adult life, she'd finally found him in Brayden. He'd been right there for years, under her very nose. She would not waste another second on doubts. They would start a life together now, and it was going to be amazing.

"Harder," she demanded.

Her inner beast wanted him wild with need when they finally came apart and claimed each other. And she was going to claim him as well. There was no doubt about that.

Brayden got on his knees, lifting her up till she was astride him, her long red hair cascading over them both. She thought she was too big for this kind of thing, but he didn't seem to think so.

Her Bear was bigger, stronger than any other man she'd ever known. He lifted her up like she weighed nothing, with firm hands on her hips and one finger teasing the crevice of her ass. He picked her up and slammed her down, impaling her on his cock over and over again. The feeling was incredible.

"Oh gods!"

Her cry echoed off the walls. But she couldn't help it. He was so deep with this new position, touching places she hadn't even known were there.

"Mine!" he roared.

Leaning forward, he took one of her nipples in his mouth while fucking her hard from below. Brayden's every drive brought her closer and closer to that pinnacle. It was just there, so close she could taste it.

Her fingers raked his shoulders, claws coming out in her wild and desperate need to come. He moved hard and fast, his own claws piercing her hips and scratching her there.

She'd be permanently marked by his animal. The knowledge that his scratches would forever be imbedded on her skin brought her that much closer to the edge.

The scent of their blood, sex, and sweat filling the air had her own fangs lengthening in response. It was primal and raw. Rough and tender. Just the way she'd dreamed it could be between fated Shifter mates.

She could only imagine the teal glow of her eyes as she gazed down at him. Her mate. He grunted and groaned, the vein in his neck throbbing as his beautiful dick slammed home.

Jessica's muscles tightened. With one final thrust, Brayden's teeth struck over her left breast just as Jessica's fangs found purchase on his opposite shoulder.

Her pussy squeezed his cock and her orgasm slammed into her hard and fast.

Fuck. Fuck. FUCK!

RRROOOAAARRRR!

Whether that was his beast or hers, she was not certain. Maybe it was both echoing inside of them. Wave after wave of pleasure grew inside of her with every pulse, grind, and thrust. Jessica thought she would die from so much of it.

She swallowed down the thick, coppery liquid from his neck and sealed the wounds with her saliva. Satisfaction at knowing he would wear her mark forever only increased her pleasure.

Brayden opened his mouth and loosed a roar that shook the fucking room. Then his lips returned to her skin, his mouth covering her mark as he sucked and licked, healing her with his saliva.

His dick pulsed as he continued to come, and she moaned in ecstasy. Jessica fucking loved the feeling she got as his thick, hot seed coated her womb and branded her as his.

They clung together through it all. Until her bones felt like jelly, and she had no strength left at all.

Still, she held on. They licked each other's wounds closed, waiting for their breath to return to normal. Finally, after several long minutes, it did.

Brayden lifted her on shaky legs and turned so they could both fall onto the bed, his cock still buried deep inside of her. She didn't want him to leave there.

Like never, ever never.

Okay, maybe when she had to pee, but that was it.

"No place else I want to be, *mate*," he growled, and she realized she'd spoken aloud.

"You're mine now," she whispered.

The words were said with reverence and awe as

she stroked his handsome face from forehead to chin.

"And you are mine, kitten. My mate, forever."

A smile broke across her face and before she knew it, he was kissing her again. It was better than what she'd describe to Uncle Uzzi. So much better than any other kiss she'd ever had or imagined.

His kiss was completely thorough, leaving nothing of her mouth or heart untouched. The soft, slow slide of his lips against hers gave way to the feel of his tongue along her seam.

He licked and nibbled, sipped, and devoured. Soft, hard, slow, then deep. He was everywhere and nowhere. So close she couldn't tell where she stopped, and he started.

She was drowning in his kiss. Happily so. When his cock pulsed and he moved once more, she couldn't stop the moan that escaped her. This time, it was no hard, desperate fucking.

This meeting was a slow slide of skin against skin. A communion of bodies and souls. She meant that in the truest sense of the word. Every single inch of Brayden was touching her.

His legs entwined with hers, his hard stomach moved in time with his thrusts along her smooth, soft one. Their arms were wrapped so tightly around each other she could barely breathe. She could only feel.

He dazzled her senses with every inch of his heated flesh. She was not just Jessica Maverick anymore. She was part of something. Part of him. And he was a part of her.

Swivel, grind, swivel, slide.

The steady thrum of his body moved in time with hers. This slow, intense fucking was a gift they gave each other, and it was more than enough to make her lose her grip on the present. Hell, she damn near lost her mind from the pleasure.

Jessica had no choice. He made her let go of every inhibition. Conquered every fear she'd ever had that maybe she wasn't good enough.

Brayden made her feel like a princess. He did not say the words. He might never. But in those moments, he showed her with his body just how he felt about her. Her heart filled with so much love for him, it only increased with every passing second and every tantalizing touch.

She might be an absolute idiot who read too much into sex and mating, but Jessica was pretty fucking sure she just fell irrevocably in love with her big Black Bear.

She opened her eyes to see his closed with

concentration as his mouth continued to do heavenly things to hers. Lifting her hands, she held his face, giving him everything she had. But she wanted more still. Rolling with him until suddenly she was on top, Jessica increased the pressure of her mouth on his.

Brayden groaned with the move. His black eyes opened, meeting hers as she continued the *swivel, grind, swivel* pace he'd set. Using her thigh muscles to squeeze him, Jessica gasped as she felt him grow harder and longer while buried deep in her weeping pussy. How was that even possible?

The rumbling growl that built up inside of him was such a fucking turn on, she increased speed. It was so fucking good. She felt her walls tighten, squeezing his dick. Brayden growled and pulled her off, turning her onto her stomach. He was behind her in a flash.

"Yes," she moaned, lifting her ass up and thrusting it out towards him.

She wanted him to fuck her like this. Her Tiger demanded it. She turned her head to see him staring at her ass, but he wasn't moving fast enough. She bucked and wiggled her hips.

"Fuck me," she demanded for the second time that night.

"Gonna take you like this, mate, then I'm gonna take this ass too," Brayden growled.

He slapped the flat of his hand against her right cheek, sending zings of pleasure straight into her pussy.

He must have liked her response because he smacked her ass again. Then he soothed it with his lips, teasing her forbidden hole with his thumbs before spreading her wide.

Jessica had never had sex back there before, but suddenly, her Tiger craved it. The animal wanted him filling her with his cum every way possible. Moisture dripped from her slit, her need out of control.

"Please," she whined, and pushed back again.

"I'll take you here later. First, I'm going to fill your pussy until my cum is dripping from you. Want that, mate?"

"Yes," she hissed.

"Whatever my mate wants," he growled, impaling her from behind.

Thank fuck.

He was so long, so hard, and so very good at fucking. Jessica moaned and gasped as he pounded into her at a punishing pace. His thick cock stroked every inch of her, spreading her wide until it almost hurt. But it was so fucking good.

He leaned forward, caging her in, and found her clit with his hand. Fucking her in long, deep strokes, Brayden brought her to orgasm in no time at all. And if that wasn't enough, he bit her again. Staking his claim one more time on her shoulder, sending another, stronger orgasm slamming into her.

"Mine," he growled.

His cock pulsed as it spewed his thick hot seed inside her already coming pussy, making it that much more intense.

Was that her third or fourth orgasm? It didn't matter to her. She'd never been so perfectly fucked in all her life. She'd never come so hard, not even with her own toys.

Jessica lost count of the number of times she came screaming his name. But she knew one thing for sure. Jessica was never letting go of her Bear.

Mine.

Forever.

Chapter Eighteen

Brayden woke to the sound of someone banging on his bedroom door. He couldn't stop a long, warning growl from escaping his lips.

His arms were full of warm, soft woman, His woman. And whoever dared interrupt them was going to have hell to pay.

Except the Neta, of course. Fuck.

"Brayden? We gotta go, bro. There's trouble. Hunter wants us ready to leave in ten," Mikey called from the hallway.

"Fuck. Alright," he growled.

"Mm, what's up?"

His sweet mate turned in his arms. His chest burned with feeling, and he thanked the universe for the gift of her one more time. He could hardly believe it was real. Damn, he was one lucky Bear.

Jessica was so fucking beautiful, sometimes it hurt to look at her. Her wild mane of red hair matched her passionate nature. Her smooth peaches and cream skin now held evidence of beard burn and bite marks, a sign she'd been well loved. By him.

Only me.

Mine, his Bear snarled.

The animal inside him had been awakened before he was ready. The beast was up now and roaring, wanting him to hunt down Mikey for pounding on his door. Brayden could not blame his animal. The Bear wanted to stay with his mate. He wanted to be buried balls deep inside her luscious heat for days on end.

Hell, maybe even for the rest of his life. Not that it was possible. But it was still a good idea.

Yesss.

"Don't know. The Neta wants me up and out," Brayden growled with regret.

"You're the Pride Beta. It's your job," she whispered, running her hands down the side of his face.

So fucking hot, he thought and leaned down to kiss her dusky rose lips. Need pulsed through him, and his dick got hard. Or maybe it was already like that.

Fuck.

Kissing her was an addiction. One he had no intention of ever giving up. The fact that she was a powerful she-Cat who went completely submissive in his arms made him insane. Even better was the way she commanded in the bedroom. It was more than he'd expected.

Better than any wet dream or fantasy he'd ever had. Jessica was hot as fuck when she told him what she wanted and practically dared him to give it to her. She was sexy and beautiful all the time, where he was concerned.

He felt his cock stir against her soft belly. Dropping kisses across her lips and chin and neck, Brayden groaned when she opened her legs. His fingers teased her already wet slit, dipping inside just slightly, then back out again to trace her lips with her own juices. She was more than ready for him.

Fuck it.

Hunter could wait.

"Need you," she moaned into his mouth and Brayden was a goner.

He kissed her again, sucking on her tongue as he

settled between her supple thighs. No better place on earth, he decided. Her ginger spiced scent combined with his until they both smelled like the heavenly mixture that would forever mark them as a mated pair.

The same way the series of bites and scratches they'd given each other the night before would announce to the entire supernatural world that Brayden and Jessica belonged together. Forever. He would rip apart anyone who thought to stand between them.

Jessica moaned, scraping her nails lovingly over the mark she'd given him on his shoulder. She traced it with her fingertips and Brayden grunted, sliding his cock into her tight, hot sheath. He almost went cross eyed from the sheer pleasure.

It would always be this way for them. Each time they had sex it would only get better. Fated mates instinctively knew ways to please each other. It was part of the magic that bound them.

Still, he wanted more. Not just sex, he wanted what her gorgeous teal eyes promised him as she moaned his name and opened her pink mouth to slide her tongue along his. He wanted her love; he realized quite suddenly.

He wanted to bury himself balls deep inside her

sweet pussy until she was carrying his cubs. Bears or Tigers, either would be fine with him. He just wanted them. Kids, a home, and family. With her. Only his sweet Jessica.

Mate.

Mine.

It didn't take long to bring them both to the brink of that sweet bliss of pure satiation. It was more like an explosion of pure emotion. Lust and need, yes, but also something else. Something deeper that he had yet to name.

He cared for her. Craved her, needed her like he needed oxygen to breathe. Loved her.

Fuck.

As his cock found heaven inside her supple body the realization dawned with blinding accuracy. He wanted her love, but he already loved her.

Loved her so much his heart nearly beat him to death just thinking about it. It wasn't always that way. Mates did not always find love. Hadn't he learned that from his past?

And yet he knew in his heart this couldn't be anything else. They both yelled their pleasure in unison. Her slick walls contracted, her pussy sucking his cum deep inside her body as she came with him.

Yes, he loved her. Deeply. Truly. Madly. And forevermore.

It was pure fact. Brayden was head over heels for his sexy little mate. He pressed one more long kiss to her lips just as another knock sounded on the door. This one threatened to break the thing down.

Fuck.

"Stop whatever the fuck you are doing and move it. The streak has attacked our Pride," Hunter roared from the hallway.

Brayden stiffened and closed his eyes. Shit. This was serious.

"Gotta go, kitten," he said and kissed her one more time.

"I know. Be safe," she returned, concern flashing in her eyes.

"Always. Stay here until I know what's going on."

"I have to open the store," she said.

"Just wait for me to check things out first. I'll call you," he insisted.

He waited until she nodded her ascent before climbing out of bed and grabbing his clothes. He wouldn't be able to concentrate if he thought she was in trouble.

After saying a quick goodbye, he left. Reluctantly, to say the least. Brayden had to make it fast. He knew if he delayed even a moment longer with another kiss or touch, he would never get out that door.

His Bear wanted to stay in his den with his mate for the rest of his days and everything else could fuck off. But he was the Beta and duty was a must. He would be honorable for his mate.

Later, he would return and pick up where he left off. The idea satisfied the beast inside, even though his chest still rumbled with his Bear's growl.

He could not help it. Brayden wanted to take her every which way again and again until the two of them could do nothing but sleep. Wrapped around each other.

Good plan.

He grunted as he hustled down the hallway to the living room, where everyone was gathered. The last thing he would have needed was Hunter breaking down his door to see him balls deep inside his sister.

Fuck.

That would have been bad. Still, he grinned to himself, unable to hide the elation he felt. And why shouldn't he feel joy?

Brayden finally had a mate. Someone of his very own to love, cherish, and protect. She was his whole world.

"Thanks for joining us," Hunter's voice dripped sarcasm, and Brayden simply nodded.

He refused to disrespect himself or his Neta with any unnecessary attitude. And he would never disrespect his mate that way. Besides, he understood. If it was his sister, he'd be pissed as well.

"The streak has entered Pride lands. They defaced some property on the outskirts of town. Breaking windows and damaging some siding on the abandoned Williams' house. Luckily, no one lives there anymore. Our sentries sent up an alert a half an hour ago. The streak was last seen on the outer edges of town in Tiger form where the forest runs into the river."

"Are we going on foot or paw?" Reg asked.

The Tiger male was young, but he had a good heart, and he was eager to prove himself. After that debacle with their former Beta, Blake, stirring up trouble, he'd turned into one of the most dependable men they had.

Brayden begrudgingly respected the man. He couldn't come right out and say it though, not after Reg had expressed some mild interest in Jessica. And there was the whole staring at her ass thing he had yet to deck the guy for. But it was coming.

Grrr, his Bear growled at the thought of any man

coveting what was his. It was a good thing he'd already marked and claimed her, or he wasn't sure he could hold back his beast.

"We'll take the trucks to the service road. Then we'll change into our fur," the Neta said.

Hunter's massive Tiger led the way through the woods with Brayden's Black Bear close to his right flank. The others surrounded them in standard tactical formation.

They would be able to defend against any attack from their enemies with fluidity and superior speed since theirs was a trained unit, and the streak was nothing more than a few misled cubs.

Brayden sniffed the air. Something was wrong. They'd been tracking the streak's movements for over three miles through the snow-covered woods.

The rogue Tiger Shifters left paw prints and clawed up trees in their wake. Not to mention a hefty amount of defecation and urine.

Fucking assholes.

It was a weak attempt to claim territory that was not theirs. Shifters rarely allowed their baser natures to run amok, but it was all these fucks seemed to know.

Hunter was not amused. He growled his displeasure for all to hear. Brayden's Bear rumbled right with him. The streak was careless, or they were purposely leaving this trail for them to follow.

Neta?

Brayden used the telepathic connection between himself and Hunter to speak to the leader of the Maverick Pride while allowing the guards with them to hear as well.

I have an uneasy feeling. I think this might be a fool's errand. These tracks are old. They have not been here for an hour at least.

Hunter paused, his teal eyes finding Brayden after a beat.

I think you're right. Let's head back to the trucks.

Hunter's Tiger loosed a mighty roar. The sound louder than any other in the forest. He used his Alpha powers to send the message.

Wherever the streak was hiding, Hunter, Brayden, and the rest of the guards were coming for them.

Grrr.

Brayden's Bear tore through the woods at a run. He was anxious and jumpy. The promise of battle had turned into a bust and now the beast wanted to check on their mate.

To make sure she'd stayed put just as he'd asked. For some reason, he doubted his sexy little mate was very good at listening. And he would enjoy spanking her for it.

Later.

First, he had to make sure she was not in harm's way. He might be new to the whole mating thing, but thousands of years of evolution could not be denied. The Bear wanted his mate now.

Mine.

"Elissa? What are you doing here? I thought Hunter told you to stay home. Especially with Reg out checking the perimeter with him," Jessica said, exasperated at finding her pregnant sister-in-law out without a guard.

"Yeah, well, this cub of ours needed his mama to stretch her legs. Seriously, I was going stir crazy by myself at the Pride House. Uncle Uzzi finished his interviews with everyone yesterday, and he left this morning for some other business."

"He did?"

"Yeah. I swear that old Witch is holding back on me. He would not tell me anything about the matches he has lined up, but he promised to come back in a few weeks. Anyway, I wanted to come on over to grab some of those *Kisses by Kylie* panties to surprise Hunter with," the Nari grinned wickedly.

Jessica snorted and walked over to the rack of delectable lingerie to show Elissa the new designs Kylie had been working on for the upcoming holiday season.

"These are full bodied and comfortable," she said, stopping when the Nari screeched excitedly.

Elissa waved a pair of crotchless blue panties and Jessica suppressed a shudder. She never, ever, wanted to picture her big brother's sexy time activities. Like ever.

Serious yuck.

"These are awesome. My mate will go crazy and look, easy access for tongue or cock," purred Elissa with one hand on her slightly swollen abdomen.

"OMG! Lissa, please, I just ate," Jessica replied, making mock barfing noises.

"Is that Elissa? Hi, girl! You like them?" Kylie called out.

The blonde she-Cat wandered out of the backroom with a measuring tape around her neck and a few sewing needles sticking out of a bob in her hands. Her wireframed glasses were perched on the end of her nose and her brown eyes sparkled with delight at the prospect of pleasing a customer.

Jessica smiled. She was happy for Kylie and couldn't wait for her lingerie to really take off. Jess was both proud and happy to be the first shop to carry her amazing creations so far.

"Hell yeah, Ky. I love them!"

Elissa gushed and swept across the room to hug the budding designer. Jessica laughed at Kylie's expression. She wasn't used to being manhandled and Elissa sometimes forgot her Alpha Shifter strength.

The little bells that hung over the front door jingled, announcing the arrival of new customers as Jessica watched Elissa drag Kylie to the back room.

She was in the middle of an enthusiastic tirade about nursing bras and, from what Jessica heard, wanted Kylie to make her a few custom improvements to the ones she'd been trying out.

Poor Kylie, once Elissa had something on her mind, there was no getting around it until it was all said and done. Jessica smiled and turned her attention to the new arrivals, her mind on the two females. She should probably call Brayden to let him know where they were, after she dealt with her customers, of course.

"Good afternoon, welcome to *Jessica's Closet*," she said, the familiar greeting dying on her lips.

Jessica's smile faltered as she took in the three huge men who'd slithered into her store. One breath told her they were Shifters, Tigers like her, but not of the Pride.

The streak.

Her she-Cat snarled, and she straightened her shoulders. Jessica fought back the fear that threatened to make itself known. Eyebrow raised, she placed her hands on her hips.

"What do you want?" she growled.

The young males all looked at each other nervously. They had expected her to cower in fear, but they were about to be disappointed. Jessica was no damsel in distress, and these young fools were going to have to learn that the hard way.

"She's a Tiger, man, but she stinks like a fucking Bear," one snarled.

He was the shortest one there, his wild eyes looked at her disgustedly and he wrinkled his nose. She barely stopped herself from hissing at him. How dare he speak of her mate that way?

"This must be that fake Neta's sister," another replied.

The male was dirty, dressed in a t-shirt and ripped jeans. His greasy blonde hair stuck up like he hadn't seen a brush in weeks as he strutted forward.

All three of them smelled like dirt and grime and bodily functions. The strength of the stench made her want to gag.

He must be the leader, she mused.

All of them had the same unkempt, disheveled look to them. Their clothes were damp, and their shoes covered in mud. They must have come through the forest. She smelled their fur on them and wondered if they'd carried their clothing with them somehow. Then she noted the backpack on the shortest one.

That one must be the pack mule.

The third was the most muscular, but still lanky. In fact, all three seemed impossibly young. Younger than she was, at any rate.

She'd heard the term *streak* once or twice and knew it was used loosely by Tiger Shifter's to describe groups of rogues who joined together for one nefarious purpose or other. Usually, to try and overthrow another male's Pride was one such reason.

If that was their aim, they were sorely mistaken. Her brother was no chump. Neither was her mate. Either of them alone would make mincemeat of this trio.

"Look," she said.

She wanted them to remain calm, thinking about Elissa and Kylie in the back room. The other two felines would have heard the commotion. Hopefully, they were calling Hunter and Brayden now.

"I think you should leave town before it is too late," she warned.

"We don't care what you think, Bear whore. Deliver a message to your brother. His time is done!"

She hissed and spun around. How had she missed a fourth rogue? The huge male was on her before she could move. His claw tipped hands wrapped around her throat and squeezed, causing her to gasp for air.

She struggled against him, clawing, and kicking, but it was no use. Either he was on something, or he was just numb to the pain she had to be causing him. Jessica fought like a hellcat. Snarls and growls filled the air, the other three Tigers shouting at their fourth, encouraging him to kill her.

She smelled his blood and knew her scratches had sliced through skin. But still, he held firm. The asshole squeezed her throat again before letting go and punching her twice in the jaw. He straddled her arms so she couldn't scratch him any longer, but she bucked and turned, doing her best to dismount him.

Motherfucker.

Her only hope was that Elissa and Kylie would

remain hidden in the back room. Of course, that was too much to ask. Just then, she heard Elissa's laughter reach the front of the shop as she and Kylie emerged into the storefront.

"Jessica! Stop you bastards!"

Elissa's gaze glittered with the gold of her she-Cat as she faced off against the four males who now stood in a circle around Jessica. The asshole who'd hit her had her up by the hair, the pain blinding her.

He growled, kicking her in the stomach, and she fell to the floor. Wind knocked out of her, she sucked in air. Fuck, it felt so good to breathe. But worry quickly overpowered her elation at being able to suck in air. Elissa had just put herself in danger.

"Lissa, run," she tried to yell, but it was no more than a hoarse cry.

"That's his bitch! The human whore the traitor took to bed. We will cleanse this joke of a Pride, starting with you," he sneered.

"Listen up, fuckwits. I'm the Nari of this Pride, and you four have a lot to answer for," snarled Elissa.

The pregnant she-Cat was trembling with rage, and Jessica had never been so fucking scared in her life. Kylie placed herself slightly in front of the Nari, and Jessica's heart really threatened to stop.

She was so small. A good ten-inches shorter than

Jessica, even shorter than the Nari herself. Yes, Kylie was born a Shifter, but these men were brutish and cruel.

They could hurt her. They could hurt them both. Fear almost stopped her heart, but she refused to give into it.

No!

Jessica had no intention of letting that happen. She had to protect her friend and her Nari. With no thought for her own self-preservation, Jessica got to her feet and jumped onto the back of the man who'd attacked her.

The other three males moved forward, shoving clothing racks out of the way, and stomping on them. Destruction and chaos seemed to be their aim. And didn't that just piss Jessica off even more?

She growled and pulled the hair of the big fucker who'd tried to hurt her. One man had made it across the store to Elissa, but Kylie jumped in front of the pregnant she-Cat. The tiny blonde shoved the Nari back and loosed her claws to scratch the bigger man.

Holy shit, Jessica thought.

Kylie was small but fast and accurate with her blows at the first. Jessica tried to keep track, but she was also fighting the biggest fucker there. He pulled her hair, swinging her head around while he tried to force her from his back.

She noticed another rogue had completed his shift, but it was too late for her to act. The animal charged Jess, knocking her off of his leader's body.

His huge claws dug into her back, and she howled in pain. Bloodied and hurt, Jessica stumbled, but regained her feet. She had no choice but to fight on. She would not stop. Thoughts of Brayden clouded her mind, and she cursed herself for going in that morning, despite his warning.

How could the universe finally give her a mate, only to take him away? She shook with anger and regret. She should have told Brayden how she felt.

Now he would never know just how much she truly loved the big Black Bear. Her thoughts were interrupted by the streak's leader who stepped into her blurry line of her vision.

"I'll show you to fuck with us, bitch," he snarled and slapped her hard across the face.

Jessica stumbled, falling to her knees. Pain erupted across her cheek and into her eye.

Fuck. That really hurt.

"You think you can just go around fucking the Bear that took Blake's position? You're nothing but a traitor to our kind," another sneered.

"You Pride Tigers think you're so much better than us. But Blake, he was one of us. He was going to take over and bring us in, after your fucking piece of shit brother wouldn't have us."

"What are you talking about? Did you ever ask Hunter about joining the Pride?" she asked, though her throat ached.

"Blake told us the truth. He told us what the so-called Neta said. Now, we're going to claim the Pride in Blake's honor, but first I am going to teach this Nari a little lesson," the big one sneered.

Jessica's heart clenched. Shit. He'd made it through Kylie to Elissa. The young Tiger's hands closed around Elissa's arm. Her eyes were wide. The scent of the Nari's fear made Jessica's she-Cat roar in fury.

"Look," she said, trying to get their attention back on her.

"Blake was a liar and an overall dickhead. You should have come to my brother. You should have asked him directly. Before touching any of his Pride, you should have done all of that. But I swear, if you touch his mate, he will not hesitate to kill you," Jessica snarled.

While she'd been talking, she'd been calling on all

her Shifter powers. She rushed the transformation and allowed her she-Cat to take charge.

Years of play fighting with her brother had made her Change one of the fastest in the Pride. Second to Hunter alone. She might be smaller than these fuckers, but she was strong, and she would not go down without a fight.

Jessica roared and watched the men pale. Only one had even started his shift, and she pinned the fucker with her jaws around his neck.

"Let Matt go," growled the man holding Elissa by the wrist.

Jessica growled louder. She wasn't doing a fucking thing until he released her. As if to prove her point, she bit harder, making the man whimper. His foul blood tainted her mouth, and she couldn't wait to spit the fucker out.

"Jess!" Elissa cried out.

At the same time, her captor shoved her away and reached into his back pocket.

"Fucking bitch," the man yelled, aiming a pistol at Jessica.

What kind of Shifter brought a gun to a Cat fight? She wanted to yowl at his lack of balls.

Weak. Pathetic.

And there wasn't anything she could do to change the outcome of what was about to happen.

Brayden. Her Tiger cried out for her mate.

I love you, Brayden. Sorry, so sorry.

She pictured her Bear in her mind. She'd die happy with him in her thoughts and in her heart. She only wished she could see him one last time to tell him face to face.

The young Tiger squeezed the trigger and time seemed to slow down. She watched the bullet rocketing towards her until it hit her.

The impact made her fly backwards, and the scent of gunpowder mixed with a fresh spray of her blood burned her nostrils.

Fuck was she angry. Her shoulder throbbed, and she felt lightheaded. She really wanted to tear the throat out of that asshole. He wasn't even a good shot.

Someone should tell people with guns that shooting is something that requires practice. Fucking jerks couldn't even do that right.

Her anger was silly, she knew. She should be happy he was a lousy shot. But she was angry and hurt. She wanted Brayden. And she wanted to beat the crap out of the piece of shit who shot her.

Before she could retaliate, the doors to the shop

burst open and a big, beautiful, and really fucking angry Black Bear charged the bastard with the gun.

Fangs, claws, and pure muscle slammed into the weaker male in a fury of motion that left her dizzy. Or maybe that was the blood loss.

Mate.

Jessica's last thought was of her gorgeous mate before she let the blackness take her.

Love you.

Chapter Twenty

When they'd left the forest and the evidence of the streak behind, something in the back of Brayden's mind urged him to go faster and he pressed down on the gas like never before.

He knew Hunter had ordered them to return to the Pride House, but something told him to pass *Jessica's Closet* first.

The second he'd jumped into his truck with Reg and Mikey dressing in the back, he'd changed direction. He was going to drive by his mate's shop before he headed to the Pride House.

It was like something was calling him there. The closer he got, the clearer it became. Something was wrong. It was Jessica. His mate was scared. Hurt maybe.

His Bear nearly erupted out of his skin before he could put the truck in park. The second he did, he jumped out of the driver's seat and into the store with his Bear bursting forth.

The scent of Jessica's blood in the air sent his Bear into a frenzy. He turned his huge, ursine head and saw the culprit. That was one sorry ass excuse for a Tiger Shifter. He just stood shaking in his boots with a gun in his hand while Brayden's Bear zeroed in on him.

This soon-to-be dead man had touched his mate. That was all the reminder his animal needed to spring into action. Saliva dripped from his fangs as he bellowed his fury. With one savage swipe of his enormous claws, he slapped the gun out of the Shifter's hands and sliced through skin and muscle like a hot knife through butter all the way to the bone.

The Tiger screamed and fell to his knees. Only the sound of Jessica's pained whimper saved him from a gory death. Instead, Brayden shifted focus onto his mate.

It would take only one move, one twist of his

hands to snap the fucker's neck like a dried twig, but he threw him to the ground instead.

Reg and Mikey had the other three rounded up and cuffed already. The Pride healer was currently tending to a Shifter female with short blonde hair.

A glance told him Elissa, his Nari, remained uninjured. She was currently kneeling over his own wounded mate, pressing a wad of material against Jessica's Tiger's shoulder.

Brayden's Bear pushed forward cautiously. With his nose, he nudged her soft reddish gold fur, breathing past the blood and pain to the ginger spiced scent he loved so much.

Please, be alright. Wake up, love.

He begged through the Pride link and their matebond.

Her Tiger was so gorgeous. But that was Jessica, a beauty in any form. Her sleek, powerful she-Cat was just as lovely as the human side of her, but he had no time to admire her.

Worry and fear pushed at him, his Bear whined and growled anxiously. He bellowed for Mikey, the Pride healer.

The Tiger did not dawdle. He ran across the store and checked over Jessica's wound. Brayden's Bear growled at the unmated male and the big man rolled his eyes.

"Change back, Brayden. I can't examine her if you're growling over me, and I have another patient," he said, sounding reasonable, though Brayden could sense his anxiety.

Fucker was right, not that Brayden would admit it. Within seconds he was a man again, crouched next to his mate's prone feline form.

"Jessica," he said her name, touching her face with hands that shook.

If anything happened to her---

No, it didn't bear thinking about.

"Nari, are you hurt?" Mikey asked their leader's mate while checking Jessica's injury.

Brayden cursed himself for not inquiring after her. Fuck. But it was all he could do to hold on to his skin while the sonovabitch who put a bullet in his mate sat crying. The Tiger was bleeding and had his mangled hands cuffed with Shifter strength resistant zip-ties behind his back on the other side of the store. He wasn't in anywhere near enough pain, according to Brayden's beast.

"I am fine," Elissa replied, interrupting his thoughts.

"Jessica was so brave. She defended us. Took the brunt of their attention."

Hunter snarled. The Neta's hands were on his mate, worry for his sister filling his gaze.

"Easy Brayden, it's a through and through," Mikey declared.

The Pride healer met his stare for a beat, then turned his head. He applied clean gauze to her wound.

"Hold this here. I have to go back to Kylie," Mikey stated, and his voice hitched a bit when he said the she-Cat's name.

Brayden almost asked him about it, but Jessica was waking up. Thank fuck.

"Will she be okay?" Elissa asked.

"She's bruised, but fine. The other female is worse off," Mikey replied.

He'd adopted a neutral tone and walked to the other woman. But Brayden had his own suspicions. Still, he pushed it away. Nothing was as important as his own mate.

"She fought them off practically alone. Broke that one's wrist before the coward over there shot her. Brayden, I am so sorry," Elissa's eyes filled with tears.

"She will be okay," Hunter whispered.

Brayden recalled how the male had come

running into the store. Within two steps he'd defeated two of the assholes, then he was on the floor with his mate in his arms, and his eyes raking over his sisters' prone form.

"Jessica's stronger than you'd think. We used to wrestle as cubs, and whenever she pinned me, I used to tell her it was because I let her, but it wasn't true. She was always badass. Don't worry, she will pull through," he murmured.

"She's been shot. These assholes put a bullet in her," Brayden snarled, trying to keep the Bear from wanting to kill everything in sight.

His beast teetered on the edge, and he finally understood the grief others felt without their mates. Maybe this happened to Valerie without John. Her choices would never sit well with him, but the Sow had not been sane without her mate.

His Bear could understand. The beast would completely takeover without Jessica in the world, bringing pain and death to all responsible.

"Come on, kitten. Come back to me," he whispered, trying to keep the fear from his voice as his she-Cat's brilliant teal eyes slowly blinked.

Her animal was still a little out of it, eyes glassy from the pain of being shot, but he saw the recognition in them. He hesitated to touch her, not wanting to cause pain. Sometimes, when the animal was more in control than the human, it was best to wait and see.

Jessica chuffed and butted him with her head, clearly happy to see him. He brought his forehead down to hers, smiling when her scratchy tongue licked his cheek. Pride in his mate filled Brayden.

Elissa gasped and cried happily, telling everyone what went down. His mate was truly fearless and brave, but he swore to gods, he would tan her hide if she ever did anything like that again.

"Hey there, Jessica. You will be fine now. I order it," he said, and Hunter's eyes flashed with emotion.

Brayden swore he could feel his Neta's powerful feelings for his family and Pride in his voice.

"Let's give them a moment," Elissa whispered, nodding at Brayden and smiling at Jessica's Tiger before allowing her mate to help her stand.

"How is Kylie?" Hunter asked.

The Alpha pair went to inquire after the young she-Cat, and to see about the prisoners.

"Kitten, you did good. I am so glad you are strong, but I need my mate," he said, stroking his mate's feline head.

He smiled at her purring and petted her soft fur with his hands.

"Yes, you were brave little she-Cat. But I need my mate's human body now. Change for me so I can care for her, please," he said earnestly.

A blink of an eye later, a naked and bloody Jessica lay before him. She groaned with the pain of her shift, hissing as the open bullet wound stitched itself together. She would need a day or so, but she would heal.

Thank the gods.

"Brayden," she rasped.

"It's okay. Don't talk now," he murmured, so overcome with emotion he was liable to break down in front of the whole fucking Pride.

Not that he gave a fuck. He was not ashamed of his love for her. She was everything, and without her, he would have nothing.

Careful of her injury, Brayden gathered her to him and lifted her up. Uncaring about his own nudity, he snagged a long piece of clothing from a nearby broken rack to cover her naked form. His Bear demanded he do so, needing to conceal her from so many eyes surrounding them.

"Brayden," she sighed again, voice raspy.

He lifted her easily off the ground. But he didn't speak. He couldn't. Not yet. Placing her in the back seat of the truck, he got in and started driving without even talking to the Neta.

He might hear shit from him later, but he'd deal with it then. For now, the Bear needed to be alone with his mate. The drive back to the Pride House only took moments. He ignored the questioning eyes of those in residence and carried his mate to his wing of the house. To his Den.

"Brayden---"

He shook his head, silencing her before she could speak. His Bear was not fully under control. As if the reality of the whole situation just dawned on him, Brayden could not trust himself to say a single word.

Instead, he set about caring for her. Walking into the large bathroom, he balanced her on his knee as he turned on the six different shower heads that faced the center of the oversized, blue-tiled shower stall. He stood her up under the warm spray and immediately joined her.

The effect was as if they were under a waterfall and soon the room was full of steam. Jessica let her head fall back as the water sluiced over her naked body. He hated the smattering of bruises that covered her. Especially the large, painful looking welt that was her bullet wound.

Knowing all evidence of her fight would be gone

by the next day did nothing to soothe his Bear. So Brayden distracted the beast. He grabbed a handful of liquid soap and began washing her body with long, slow rubs of his oversized hands.

"Feels good," she whispered, and leaned into his touch.

Fuck, he loved her like this.

Soft and pliant in his arms. The thought of almost losing her sent his animal into a frenzied rage. He closed his eyes, allowing his beast to feel the truth of her beneath his hands. She was here, alive, and well, and his.

Brayden ignored the throbbing of his cock and set about washing the blood and scent of battle off his beautiful, brave mate.

"Brayden," she purred his name, touching his shoulders lightly, as if to steady herself.

He would always be there to support her, to hold her up. It was his privilege, as well as his duty. Brayden's breathing grew heavy as he added more soap and lifted his arms to shampoo her mass of hair.

Gods, he loved her hair. It was like holding fire. So beautiful and different from anything he'd ever held. He loved her peaches and cream skin that was slowly revealed after he'd washed away the blood and gore. Upon rinsing the shampoo from her hair, he added conditioner and repeated the process.

Caring for her soothed his beast. Still, he didn't trust himself to talk. How could he explain what he was feeling to her? How could she ever know how much she meant?

"I'm sorry, mate," she said.

"I love you."

Her declaration held so much heat, it was enough to have him lift his eyes to her questioning ones. Desire scented the air, his and hers mixed. He couldn't help it. His mate was nude and in his arms. How could he not want her?

Without planning it, Brayden pulled Jessica towards him and crushed her against his chest. Tremors wracked his body as he pressed her close. Something between a sob and a roar tore out of his throat as he held his precious mate to him for all he was worth.

He could barely catch his breath. Couldn't stop the raging tide of emotion from leaking out.

"Mate," he said, repeating the word over and over.

His voice hoarse with worry and fear, and love. So much love.

"I'm okay. I'm fine. Brayden, I'm here with you."

He felt her arms, the strength in them as she hugged him back, whispering words of comfort and support.

Brayden stopped trembling for a moment, unashamed by his display of feeling. He was a Shifter and a man. He would never apologize for the way he felt.

Picking his head up, he looked into her tear-filled eyes and his heart contracted in his chest. Her blue depths reflected his own epiphany right back at him and his hearts swelled.

Brayden ignored the tears that leaked from his eyes, his emotions just too powerful to contain. He'd found his one true mate, and he'd almost lost her today.

"Jessica, I know I haven't said the words yet, but I need to tell you, I love-"

"I love you too," she said before he could get the words out.

He laughed through the pain and tears of his almost loss. She smiled up at him, the bruise on her cheek had turned an ugly shade of yellow, but it did nothing to mar her beauty.

She was radiant. His own personal sun, bringing warmth and light to his life.

"Jessica Maverick, I love you so fucking much,"

he growled the words and crashed his mouth to hers.

This was a kiss he never wanted her to forget. He wanted to stamp it on her very soul, the way it would forever be ingrained upon his.

He poured his love, his esteem, his unyielding respect, and undying devotion into this one act. Swallowing her tears, he vowed to never make her cry again. Not with anything but love.

Fuck, she loved him. The knowledge made him feel ten-feet tall. Invincible, like he could do anything.

Brayden fed off her mouth, licking her lips and teasing her tongue. He traced every inch of the warm cavern, including gums and teeth. He wanted every bit of her to carry some memory of him. She was his. Every single inch.

Mine.

<h1 style="text-align:center">Epilogue</h1>

essica moaned into Brayden's mouth as he lifted her out of the shower and walked them both to his bed.

She dearly loved his bed. It was big and comfortable, not too hard, and not too soft.

Every inch was *purrfect*.

Just like her mate.

"Jessica," he growled her name.

Her big, sexy mate settled between her splayed legs, sucking, and nibbling on her nipples before sliding down to feast on her sex. She was so fucking glad her mate was a Bear and that he craved a certain brand of honey.

Namely hers.

Sighing into his touch, she allowed herself to just

feel as Brayden started with long, slow swipes of his tongue.

She bucked her hips, encouraging him to move faster, but he wouldn't be rushed. It seemed the day's earlier incident had left him with a vengeful side.

He had told her not to go out, and she went, anyway. And now he was going to torture her by keeping her orgasm just out of reach.

Ooh, the jerk!

Sigh.

But damn, that felt good. So very good.

Maybe it paid to be bad once in a while. Especially if oral sex was the way he planned on punishing her.

Well, what was she supposed to do all day, just sit around waiting? Not her.

She was an independent woman. A Shifter to boot. They'd just have to work out the particulars of their relationship later. When she could think again.

"Oh gods," she moaned just as he added two thick fingers to the mix, spearing her on his digits as he suckled her nub.

Her stomach tightened with impending ecstasy, only to tremble with unfulfillment as he stilled his movements.

Grrr.

"What do you need, baby?"

"Move, please do something," she growled and bucked her hips.

Her she-Cat snarled, eager for him to finish what he'd started. She wanted him balls deep, pounding into her, rubbing his scent on her as he fucked her stupid.

"I will. In time. You are so fucking sweet and all mine," he growled, smiling wickedly as he placed one open-mouthed kiss to her pussy.

He dipped his tongue to lightly tease her nub. Those fucking lips of his were driving her insane. It might be decidedly un-feminist to be reduced to a blathering idiot because of one man's sexual prowess, but Jessica did not give one single fuck.

Her mate was hotter than hell and he was welcome to reduce her to nonverbal gibberish anytime. And hopefully, that was often.

"I'm gonna make you come, kitten. Then I'm gonna fill you with my cock. I'm gonna fuck you so damn good, you won't know where you end, and I begin. Want that, kitten?"

"Yes, fuck yes, please," she whimpered, and nodded as moisture dripped from her slit down to the sheets.

Fuck it. They'd wash. She was too wrapped up in

the sensual haze her mate had created to care. Emotions raged in a tsunami within her.

Possession.

Desire.

Need.

And Love.

Most of all love, pulsed throughout her entire body. The thoughts were loud and strong, echoing in her heart and mind until she realized they weren't just her thoughts.

They were Brayden's.

He settled into a rhythm with his mouth on her sex. One thing became clear to her even as she fell under the spell of his lovemaking. Her sexy mate was broadcasting his thoughts and feelings.

A true matebond had been formed during their claiming. She could hear him now, feel him inside, which was so much more than the average Pride connection.

She could feel his true emotions for her. Especially when they were like this. And he did love her. The pure, honest emotion erupted from him like a volcano as he made love to her.

Not just fucking.

Never just that.

Loving on you. Always love.

Love, kitten. So fucking much love.

She felt it as sure as she felt her heart squeeze to bursting with love for him. Pride and joy filled her as the ripples of her orgasm began.

He made her feel desired, like no other. Wanted, protected, cherished, and sexy as sin. The sounds of his growling moans as he flicked his tongue over her nub one last time before she exploded almost sent her over the edge alone.

"I need you," he grunted, and placed the head of his thick cock at her heated entrance.

But instead of pushing inside like she so desperately wanted, he teased her slit with his broad head. Up and down, he swiped, reducing her to a mass of quivering, shuddering moans, and sighs with every nudge of his dick along her hardened little bundle of nerves.

"Brayden."

Jessica wanted him so fucking much. He brought his head even with hers, tracing her lips with his tongue the same way his cock traced her slit. Then, at the same time his tongue entered her mouth, his hips thrust, and he slid deep within her channel.

Jessica sighed with pure pleasure. Rocking her hips, she cradled him with her thighs, loving the feel of her big, strong mate as he filled both her mouth and her sex.

"Jessica," his gravelly voice rumbled.

The sound going into her open mouth as she continued to kiss and lick him in between groans.

"Love you. Love my mate," he growled, increasing speed and pressure.

She hissed as he ground his pubis into her cleft as he set a furious pace for their lovemaking. Sweat coated their bodies, the sounds of their flesh coming together was like a symphony to her ears. She felt her orgasm begin.

Too soon, but too good to hold off. With any luck, he'd fall off the edge with her and then they could start all over again. The more Brayden pumped, the more she wanted his cum coating her walls. His thick, veined cock stroked every inch of her sheath, hitting that one secret spot no man had ever touched.

Little electric tendrils of pleasure began sparking and traveling through her body until she was a living, breathing mass of feeling. And all she could feel was him.

"Love you, Brayden," she moaned as her sex clamped down on his shaft.

"Fuck, kitten, do you even know how good it

feels to be in you? To feel your pussy sucking my dick is pure fucking heaven," he grunted.

"As good as it feels to have you in me," she returned as he thrust one, two, three times a charm and roared his completion just as fireworks burst behind her eyelids.

The entire world went silent for a moment as the most intense pleasure Jessica had ever felt filled her entire being.

"That was amazing," she exclaimed, or, *er*, she would have if she could stop gasping for air.

"No, kitten," he disagreed.

"You are the amazing one."

Taking her face in both his hands, Brayden lowered his mouth to hers. He was such an incredible kisser. Why was it she forgot that until his lips were on hers?

She might have just touched heaven in her mate's arms, but that mouth of his had a way of igniting infernos in her blood. Arousal grew again. Deep inside her, and she knew it would only ever continue to grow for him. Her mate.

Brayden grunted, a deep rumbling sound that reverberated through her body and still his mouth remained fastened to hers. That long, slick tongue of his grazed over hers, rubbing and caressing it tenderly between the sweet, tantalizing brushes of his expert lips.

His beard felt good in her hands as she raised them to caress his handsome face. He was so good looking, so good in bed, and for the first time in her life, Jessica felt whole. Then the reason for it all came to her.

"Oh my gods," she said, and giggled against his mouth.

"What?"

"You kissed me!"

"Um, Jess, I've been kissing you nonstop for two days now?"

He looked as though he questioned her sanity. He brushed her hair behind her ear. The act of tenderness touching her inside her heart.

"No, you *kissed me.*"

She looked at him, waiting for him to comprehend.

Ugh, men!

"Brayden, you kissed me, and it was perfect. I've finally been *purrfectly kissed,*" she practically screamed it to the world.

Hell, she wanted to, but then he'd probably really question her sanity.

Instead, her *purrfect* mate just laughed along with her.

"Jess?"

"Yeah?"

"I'm not finished yet," he growled, black eyes glittering with promise.

Then her sinfully delicious Black Bear leaned forward, and she practically squealed with delight.

Brayden gifted her with another purrfect kiss.

Then he did it again. And again.

And again...

E*lsewhere...*

Back in his own apartment, Uzzi Stregovich of the infamous Uncle Uzzi's Magical Matchmaking Service was sitting at his desk with a delicious cup of tea and one of the special cookies the Nari of the Maverick Pride had sent home with him. He was really getting the hang of his computer and had just read a rather interesting email. His magic buzzed around him as he reread the missive.

Dear Uncle Uzzi,

My name is Gretchen Kaepernick. I am Elissa

Phoenix-Maverick's former roommate, and I am moving to Maverick Point to take over Mrs. Bowers' lease.

I've always wanted to run my own salon, and this is a fantastic opportunity. Everything is in perfect order, so I literally just have to move in. Everything will be up and running just after the new year.

Now to the point of this email. You see, I haven't had much luck with men in forever and I was wondering if you could arrange for me to meet a nice one? I am a bigger than average girl and I don't want to settle.

It is true, I can come on a bit strong and, okay, well, I'm just plain blunt when it comes to how I feel. Elissa tells me I am too frank, but I can't help it. I turn all my dates away with talk of wanting a future and a family someday. But it's true. It's what I want.

Elissa told me to contact you about maybe helping me find my own happily-ever-after? So what do you think? Can you help me, Uncle Uzzi?

Thank you for your consideration,

Gretchen

Well, thought Uncle Uzzi. Things were about to get even more interesting in Maverick Point. He wondered if this little human, who did not know of Shifters, would be open to the possibility of being the fated mate of a man who also turned into a beast.

Hmmm.

Interesting.

Uncle Uzzi smiled as he sifted through notes he'd taken when he'd visited the Pride House.

This one, he thought, and felt his liebling's presence. Ah! If Betty approved, then Uzzi was correct.

This Tiger was the one for the unknowing normal. He smiled, pleased with himself.

Poor little pussy did not know what he was getting himself into. Uzzi only hoped the Tiger could handle it.

"Well done, liebling," he said as his beloved's essence departed once more.

He would join her someday, but until then, he had matches to make.

T *he end...*

P.S

Don't forget to tell me how you liked this story by leaving your honest review!

No pressure. 😉

A review can be one or two brief sentences where you simply state whether you enjoyed the story and would recommend it to someone! It is an enormous help to authors and the best way for us to reach larger audiences so we can keep writing the stories you love!

Thank you so much!

Xoxo!

Del mare alla stella,

C.D. Gorri

Beware... Here Be Dragons!

The Falk Clan Tales began as my stories surrounding four dragon Brothers and how they find their one true mates, but when a long lost brother arrives on the scene, followed by a few more Shifters…what can I say? The more the merrier!

Each Dragon's chest is marked with his rose, the magical link to his heart and his magic. They each have a matching gemstone to go with it.

She's given up on love, but he's just begun.

In *The Dragon's Valentine* we meet the eldest Falk brother, Callius. He is on a mission to find a Castle and his one true mate, one he can trust with his diamond rose….

His heart is frozen; can she change his mind about love?

In *The Dragon's Christmas Gift* our attention shifts to Alexsander, the youngest brother of the four. He has resigned himself to a life alone, until he meets *her*.

Some wounds run deep, can a Dragon's heart be unbroken?

The Dragon's Heart is the story of Edric Falk who has vowed never to love again, but that changes when he meets his feisty mate, Joselyn Curacao.

She just wants a little fun, he's looking for a lifetime.

We finally meet Nikolai Falk and his sexy Shifter mate in *The Dragon's Secret*.

Now available in a boxed set.

Guess what…. I've got more Dragons on the way!

Look for The Dragon's Treasure now available, and the upcoming The Dragon's Dream and The Dragon's Surprise!

Other Titles by C.D. Gorri

Young Adult Urban Fantasy Books:

Wolf Moon: A Grazi Kelly Novel Book 1

Hunter Moon: A Grazi Kelly Novel Book 2

Rebel Moon: A Grazi Kelly Novel Book 3

Winter Moon: A Grazi Kelly Novel Book 4

Chasing The Moon: A Grazi Kelly Short 5

Blood Moon: A Grazi Kelly Novel 6

*Get all 6 books NOW AVAILABLE IN A BOXED SET:

The Complete Grazi Kelly Novel Series

Casting Magic: The Angela Tanner Files 1

Keeping Magic: The Angela Tanner Files 2

G'Witches Magical Mysteries Series

Co-written with P. Mattern

G'Witches

G'Witches 2: The Hary Harbinger

<u>*Paranormal Romance Books:*</u>

<u>*Macconwood Pack Novel Series:*</u>

Charley's Christmas Wolf: A Macconwood Pack Novel 1

Cat's Howl: A Macconwood Pack Novel 2

Code Wolf: A Macconwood Pack Novel 3

The Witch and The Werewolf: A Macconwood Pack Novel 4

To Claim a Wolf: A Macconwood Pack Novel 5

Conall's Mate: A Macconwood Pack Novel 6

Her Solstice Wolf: A Macconwood Pack Novel 7

Werewolf Fever: A Macconwood Pack Novel 8

Also available in 2 boxed sets:

The Macconwood Pack Volume 1

The Macconwood Pack Volume 2

<u>*Macconwood Pack Tales Series:*</u>

Wolf Bride: The Story of Ailis and Eoghan A Macconwood Pack Tale 1

Summer Bite: A Macconwood Pack Tale 2

His Winter Mate: A Macconwood Pack Tale 3

Snow Angel: A Macconwood Pack Tale 4

Charley's Baby Surprise: A Macconwood Pack Tale 5

Home for the Howlidays: A Macconwood Pack Tale 6

A Silver Wedding: A Macconwood Pack Tale 7

Mine Furever: A Macconwood Pack Tale 8

A Furry Little Christmas: A Macconwood Pack Tale 9

Also available in two boxed sets:

The Macconwood Pack Tales Volume 1

Shifters Furever: The Macconwood Pack Tales Volume 2

The Falk Clan Tales:

The Dragon's Valentine: A Falk Clan Novel 1

The Dragon's Christmas Gift: A Falk Clan Novel 2

The Dragon's Heart: A Falk Clan Novel 3

The Dragon's Secret: A Falk Clan Novel 4

The Dragon's Treasure: A Falk Clan Novel 5

Dragon Mates: The Falk Clan Series Boxed Set Books 1-4

The Bear Claw Tales:

Bearly Breathing: A Bear Claw Tale 1

Bearly There: A Bear Claw Tale 2

Bearly Tamed: A Bear Claw Tale 3

Bearly Mated: A Bear Claw Tale 4

Also available in a boxed set:

The Complete Bear Claw Tales (Books 1-4)

The Barvale Clan Tales:

Polar Opposites: The Barvale Clan Tales 1

Polar Outbreak: The Barvale Clan Tales 2

Polar Compound: A Barvale Clan Tale 3

Polar Curve: A Barvale Clan Tale 4

Also available in a boxed set:

The Barvale Clan Tales (Books 1-4)

<u>*Barvale Holiday Tales:*</u>

A Bear For Christmas

Hers To Bear

Thank You Beary Much

Also available in a boxed set:

The Barvale Holiday Tales (Books 1-3)

<u>*Purely Paranormal Romance Books:*</u>

Marked by the Devil: Purely Paranormal Romance Books

Mated to the Dragon King: Purely Paranormal Romance Books

Claimed by the Demon: Purely Paranormal Romance Books

Christmas with a Devil, a Dragon King, & a Demon: Purely Paranormal Romance Books

Vampire Lover: Purely Paranormal Romance Books

Grizzly Lover: Purely Paranormal Romance Books

Elvish Lover: Purely Paranormal Romance Books

Hot Dire Wolf Nights: Purely Paranormal Romance Books

Christmas With Her Chupacabra: Purely Paranormal Romance Books

<u>*The Wardens of Terra:*</u>

Bound by Air: The Wardens of Terra Book 1

Star Kissed: A Wardens of Terra Short

Waterlocked: The Wardens of Terra Book 2

Moon Kissed: A Wardens of Terra Short

**Now in a boxed set and in audio!*

<u>*The Maverick Pride Tales:*</u>

SERIES MAKEOVER COMING SOON

<u>*Dire Wolf Mates:*</u>

SERIES MAKEOVER COMING SOON

<u>*Wyvern Protection Unit:*</u>

SERIES MAKEOVER COMING SOON

<u>*Standalones:*</u>

The Enforcer

Blood Song: A Sanguinem Council Book

<u>*EveL Worlds:*</u>

Chinchilla and the Devil: A FUCN'A Book

Sammi and the Jersey Bull: A FUCN'A Book

Mouse and the Ball: A FUCN'A Book

<u>*The Guardians of Chaos:*</u>

Wolf Shield: Guardians of Chaos Book 1

Dragon Shield: Guardians of Chaos Book 2

Stallion Shield: Guardians of Chaos Book 3

Panther Shield: Guardians of Chaos 4

Witch Shield: Guardians of Chaos 5

<u>*Howl's Romance*</u>

Mated to the Werewolf Next Door: A Howl's Romance

The Tiger King's Christmas Bride

Claiming His Virgin Mate: Howls Romance

<u>*Twice Mated Tales*</u>

Doubly Claimed

Doubly Bound

Doubly Tied

<u>*Hearts of Stone Series*</u>

Shifter Mountain: Hearts of Stone 1

Shifter City: Hearts of Stone 2

Shifter Village: Hearts of Stone 3

<u>*Accidentally Undead Series*</u>

Fangs For Nothin'

<u>*Moongate Island Tales*</u>

Moongate Island Mate

<u>*Mated in Hope Falls*</u>

Mated by Moonlight

<u>*Speed Dating with the Denizens of the Underworld*</u>

Ash: Speed Dating with the Denizens of Underworld

Arachne: Speed Dating with the Denizens of Underworld

<u>*Hungry Fur Love*</u>

Hungry Like Her Wolf: Magic and Mayhem Universe

<u>*Shifters Unleashed Boxed Sets*</u>

Check out these amazing anthologies where you can find some of my books and the works of other awesome authors!

Midnight Magic Anthology (Water Witch)

Rituals & Runes Anthology (Air Witch)

<u>*Island Stripe Pride*</u>

Tiger Claimed

<u>*NYC Shifter Tales*</u>

Cuff Linked

Sealed Fate

<u>*A Howlin' Good Fairytale Retelling*</u>

Sweet As Candy (as seen in Once Upon An Ever After)

<u>*Coming Soon:*</u>

If The Shoe Fits: A Howlin' Good Fairytale Retelling

Spring Fling (co-written with P. Mattern)

For Fangs Sake

Tiger Denied

Moongate Island Captive

Hungry For Her Bear: Magic and Mayhem Universe

The Dragon's Surprise

The Dragon's Dream

Bearing Gifts

Taming Magic: The Angela Tanner Files 3

Vampire Shield: Guardians of Chaos 6

Chickee and the Paparazzi: FUCN'A

The Wolf's Winter Wish: A Macconwood Pack Tale

The Hybrid Assassin

How the fuck did I wind up here?

It was all Elissa could do not to slam her face down on the table as she pondered that question for the umpteenth time since leaving her cozy Hoboken apartment to go on this so called date.

"So, babe," the over-stuffed, heavily-cologned, and downright fugly man said.

Her date of the evening looked like something out of a bad sitcom as he tried to lean over the stained tablecloth of the rundown hotel buffet room, he'd driven two hours to get to. Waggling his caterpillar-like eyebrows, he gave her the once over and Elissa's skin crawled.

Oh, hell no.

"I got a room upstairs, you know, for *after*," he

told her, nodding his head, and biting his lower lip in a manner she assumed he thought was provocative.

At best, it was nauseating.

FML.

How was this guy Elissa's date for the evening? What had she done to deserve this?

Little Gianni. Yup, that was how he'd introduced himself. And here she was. On a blind date with a guy who had the word 'little' in front of his name.

Well, what did she expect? Roses and champagne? In this economy? She didn't know where Cinder-fucking-ella got her prince, but it sure as fuck wasn't in Jersey.

Elissa could only blame herself for agreeing to go on this blind date. Initially, the whole Little Gianni fiasco had been intended for her roommate.

Wait a second. Scratch that thought.

It *was* all Gretchen's fault. That ungrateful cow!

She tried to play it off like she was some sweet little homegrown maiden. Oh, just wait till Elissa got home. Gretchen was never going to hear the end of it.

She owed Elissa. Big time. Like a whole month of washing the dishes big time. The rat trap they shared in her hometown of Hoboken was all the two women could afford, and for the most part, they got along just fine.

In fact, they'd grown to be close friends over the three years they'd lived together. It was the only reason she'd ever agreed to this date from Hell.

Elissa sighed and looked over at Little Gianni. Maybe he wasn't all that bad?

"*BEEEELLLLLLLLCHHH!* 'Scuse me, doll. Better out, am I right?"

Gianni winked and Elissa wished for a black hole to open up and swallow her up right through the floor.

OMFG.

The man just burped out loud like he was in a frat boy belting contest, only those days passed him up about thirty years ago.

For fuck's sake. Gretchen, you so owe me.

Elissa cursed her roommate and tried not to groan. But Little Gianni wasn't quite done. The grown ass man lifted his leg and let one rip.

Right. Fucking. There.

Elissa was going to die before the end of the night.

Literally.

This is what you get when you do a friend a favor without asking for details! Idiota!

The voice of her Italian grandmother sounded in her brain. She tried to ignore it, willing herself not to wince at the man while he sucked air, and who knows what else, noisily through his coffee-stained teeth.

Ew. So gross.

That was the perfect word to describe it. The only word, in fact. The entire date was just so fucking gross. She still couldn't believe her sweet little roommate from Iowa, *Gretchen Kaepernick,* she of the wispy hair and baby blues, had set her up with this guy!

What the actual fuck was up with that?

Little Gianni was a slob. Actually, he looked just like her Uncle Nico, and that was not a good thing. Seriously, not good at all.

He wore his hair slicked back in a too tight pony-tail that emphasized his rapidly receding hairline. As if that wasn't enough to put her off, he was sporting an enormous paunch. Now, being a curvy girl, Elissa appreciated food and was in no way against men showing the same appreciation.

She liked bigger men. Always had. But bigger did not mean you had to be sloppy. Little Gianni's stomach was literally hanging out from under a tight tan golf shirt that had definitely seen better days.

The man didn't even look like he had ever played a sport of any kind. With it, he wore brown polyester pants that were three inches above his ankles and unbuttoned at the waist.

He didn't look like he tried at all for this date. What kind of guy did that? His shirt collar was bent and wrinkled, and all three buttons were open to his chest, revealing a mat of oily, dark hair and pimples.

Somehow, he'd managed to tuck the back of the shirt in, but the front simply would not hold in that stomach. What worried her more were the tight brown pants.

As he sat back and stretched, she wondered if she should take cover. They looked like they were one bite from exploding off his body. Elissa shuddered at the image.

Please God, if You have an ounce of mercy, don't let that happen, she prayed.

"Hang on, doll, I gotta take this," he said, and turned to answer his cell phone.

It was ringing to the tune of '70s disco music she hadn't heard since the last family reunion. Her eyes kept going to the huge stain on the front of his shirt. It was a little game she liked to call *what the hell is that.*

Coffee, she guessed.

"Up your ass, Bruno. I gotta have it by Monday," he cursed into the receiver.

Elissa winced at the spectacle he was making of them both. There were only a handful of people there, but still.

Deep breaths.

Ew. Maybe not.

She coughed as the strong body spray, that he'd obviously used a ton of in lieu of a shower, bad move in her opinion, invaded her lungs.

Oh, this was so bad.

Elissa was, by no means, a snob. But this guy looked like he'd stepped out of a bad 1980s mafia spoof film. What's worse, he kept smacking his lips together as he hung up the phone and looked her over from head to chest.

Thank fuck for the table, she thought, wishing she could hide her bosoms from his view.

"Ssssss," he hissed, like it was sexy or something.

She just grimaced. Elissa might be able to forgive a lot of quirks, but she hated mouth noises. Really hated them. It was a super pet peeve of hers. Never mind his totally inappropriate and unwelcomed leer.

She started counting the minutes, willing the date to be over already. Plenty of people would tell her she shouldn't be so choosy, but really? She was not this desperate.

Not yet anyway.

So, she was curvy and a little mouthy too. But was it wrong to want a man with good table manners? Even if men were thin on the ground for someone like her.

As a chef, she'd worked in a lot of restaurants and even as a personal cook for professional couples. She'd seen her fair share of unhappy couples and downright uncomfortable marriages. But as far as she was concerned, all relationships went downhill when good table manners were dismissed.

Good manners were merely a sign that a person was thoughtful and respectful. At least, that was what Nonna had told her. Gianni here had clearly missed that lesson as a child. Elissa had to work not to groan in disgust as he slurped a raw clam down his gullet.

Shudder.

Was there no end to his feeding? That's what it reminded her of. Feeding time at the zoo.

OMG. That was rude, she scolded herself. But it wasn't like she said it out loud.

All she wanted to do was go home. At least she was comfortable. *She'd* worn her softest pair of black leggings for this disaster date, paired with one of her favorite tunics on top.

It was dark green with tiny black buttons down the front and showed just the right amount of cleavage. She'd gone for neat and tidy as opposed to downright sexy.

Good call, in her opinion. Elissa looked perfectly fine for a nice *getting to know you* dinner, which is what she thought she was getting when her roommate asked her to step in for her on a blind date that one of her best client's had set up for her.

Elissa shuddered now, thinking how good old Gianni here would've reacted to the red dress and heels she'd contemplated before checking the weather report.

Gulp.

The lewd man was already salivating, and she was so not having it. Fending off his unwanted advances was not how she wanted to finish the night.

Ew again.

Elissa shivered, slightly chilled despite the fact they were indoors. It was a cold, gloomy evening, and the forecast called for even more rain later that night. Not at all unusual for this time of year in the Garden State.

November was always chilly in the evenings, rainy too. Elissa tended to run warm, but she was glad she'd brought a jacket with her. Especially since her date refused to turn the heat on in the car.

When she'd asked, he'd looked offended and told her it wasted gas.

Um. Okay.

She checked her phone. It was only seven o'clock, but the two hour drive was still ahead of them. Maybe they could make it home before ten if they left soon.

Ugh. Did he just blow his nose?

"Allergies, doll. Say, you gonna eat that?" he asked before scooping a fry from her dish and swallowing it down.

Elissa was gonna kill her roomie. Gretchen was a hair and nail stylist. A lot of her clients were elderly, and they just loved her. They were always offering to set her up on blind dates with their nephews and grandsons.

Mostly, the sweet old ladies were kind. They swore they could find her curvy roommate the right man, assuming she was single because she was new to town. Well, when Elissa got home tonight, she was going to tell Gretchen she needed to fire the old lady who set this date up from being her client.

Like *ASAP*.

No one who liked Gretchen would've sent her out with this guy. Gianni reached over and touched her hand and Elissa pulled back, reaching for the napkin.

Gross.

"I sure hope you ain't a cold one, doll," he said, shaking his head.

"What?"

"Ain't gonna matter. I know just what you need, doll."

She was still wiping the greasy residue he'd transferred to her skin from the food he ate sans utensils. This was too much. Elissa was beyond uncomfortable with all the leering and bad attempts at innuendo.

Plus, she was starving. One look at the dump he'd taken her to, and she knew she could never eat there. The chef in her wouldn't allow it.

To think they drove two hours for this! She'd practically frozen to death in his maroon Cadillac, listening to a CD of the Rat Pack, while Gianni crooned loudly, and off key, to the music.

Normally, she was a fan of the famous group of legendary singers. Having grown up in Hoboken, she couldn't not be a Sinatra fan. Though, to be honest, Dean Martin had always been her favorite.

Still, Elissa was a firm believer that there were just some people you did not try to imitate. Especially not if you were Little Gianni. While he was belting his heart out, he'd been trying to get his right hand on her thigh. She'd asked him politely to stop.

Twice.

Then she'd been forced to try something a little more drastic. Like spilling her hot tea on the offending hand the third time he'd tried it. Finally, he'd removed his hand from her leg. Not making a fourth attempt, which she was grateful for.

Elissa should've taken that behavior as a sign and gotten out of the car. But no. She'd wanted to do Gretchen a solid. So, against her better judgement, she gave the creep another chance.

Idiota, her grandmother's voice echoed in her brain again.

The old woman had loved her. Elissa knew that without a doubt. She'd raised her after her own parents had passed on in a tragic automobile accident when Elissa was just twelve.

Her grandmother was a no-nonsense kind of lady who dished out priceless wisdom with brutally honest insights. It was the same way she dished out huge bowls of pasta with her amazing meatballs and homemade sauce. Not to mention a side order of back-breaking hugs that Elissa still missed.

Nonna cooked like that all the time. She made a huge pot of sauce every weekend, and she was happy to serve it to Elissa and her teammates and friends, especially after games and tournaments.

Soccer had been her sport of choice, and cooking had soon become her favorite hobby. Her grandmother had encouraged her in both pursuits. Guiding her in one and cheering her on in the other. Elissa still missed her terribly.

"Hey babe, ain't you gonna eat nothin'? You know they charge twenty dollars just to sit down," Little Gianni interrupted her train of thought.

Elissa was forced to turn her mind back to the present, which unfortunately included watching, *and hearing,* him as he sucked on his teeth and stuffed another breaded shrimp down his throat.

"I'm fine," she answered with a polite smile plastered on her face.

Just get home, Lissa. Just get him to take you home.

Elissa closed her eyes when he looked back down at his dish. Thank God for small favors, she mused. At least he was more interested in eating at the moment.

He'd taken her to the rattiest looking hotel and casino she'd ever seen in her life. And the buffet room?

Ew.

Seriously, the place had to be violating at least a dozen health codes. When Gianni had said Atlantic City, she'd thought at least the atmosphere would be exciting. But they were so far from the real glitz and entertainment, they might as well be anywhere else.

She sighed, looking at the plate she'd made for herself. Elissa couldn't even fake an interest in the food. As a chef, it was hard enough to dine out.

She was always judging the food, the service, the ingredients. How could she not? It was her business. And that was when the food was good!

This was not good. Not at all.

She'd been to hospitals that served better food. Old yellow lights buzzed and blinked around the buffet, giving it an abandoned kind of feel. The menu was made up of mostly frozen then fried or baked cuisine.

Reheated actually. It was like a giant TV dinner buffet where every item was previously frozen when already cooked and warmed up in an oven.

It was the kind of food sold cheap at restaurant

supply stores in bulk. Yeah, this was much worse than hospital food, in her opinion.

There was a worn carpet on the floor, a handful of scattered tables in the dining room, elevator music on in the background, and the entire place smelled like canned soup.

Not to mention not one of the five people there besides them was under sixty years old.

"Gianni," she said, leaning forward so as not to hurt his feelings.

"I thought you mentioned something about seeing a show tonight. Is it here?"

Please don't be here.

If he was taking her somewhere else, she could beg off and hire a cab to take her home. There was no way she was sitting through anything else with this man. Not now. Not ever.

"Ah, I see, babe, you want some entertainment first, I get it," he snickered loudly, and she blanched.

Whatever he thought was going to happen wasn't. She needed to disabuse him of the notion, and fast.

"Alright, alright. Lemme finish this, babe. Then we'll go up to the room I got for us," he said.

Before she could make sense of the ludicrous statement, he slurped another fried shrimp, don't ask how. Then he grabbed her arm and yanked her from the seat before she could even react.

Elissa tugged on his hold, but the man was immovable. Tossing a five-dollar bill on the table, Little Gianni snatched a toothpick from the hostess stand before dragging her outside.

Great, he was a cheap tipper, too.

All she wanted was to go home. Figuring the best way to do that would probably be to get him to the car, she let him lead the way.

Once inside, she would ask him to drive back to Hoboken so she could wring Gretchen's neck. Fuming, she pulled her arm out of his hand and walked behind him.

The rain was really pouring, and the cheap bastard had refused valet. Elissa ducked her head so she wouldn't get so wet. Of course, the jacket she'd brought was light and had no hood.

Gianni had an umbrella, but he didn't offer to hold it for her, and honestly, she did not relish the idea of getting any closer to him than necessary.

Seriously, not happening.

Now all she had to do was break the news. She had no intention of watching a show or returning to the hotel with him.

What could go wrong?

Excerpt from *Wolf Shield: Guardians of Chaos*

What a day! Fergie McAndrews headed towards the pick-up truck she'd borrowed from her roommate for work that morning.

Of course, the thirty-thousand dollar certified used luxury car she'd splurged on earlier in the year was in the shop. Again.

Just another in a long line of bad decisions. After leaving a perfectly good job for a startup company, she was laid off three weeks ago and had to borrow money from her parents to pay rent. Wasn't that humiliating?

"This is the last time, Ferg," her step-monster had said after she'd Venmo'd the money to her.

God forbid the mechanic call and tell her the car

was ready. She wouldn't be able to pick it up for another week. That was when she got her first paycheck from her newest gig at L-Corp. Not a startup, but an older company with new offices in Bayonne, which was only a half-hour commute.

But to commute, you needed a car. Fergie had no choice but to borrow the old pick-up from her best friend and roommate, Jessenia Banks. It wasn't like she needed the truck. She worked from home these days. Besides, Fergie promised to fill it up and have it washed.

She huffed out a breath. It'd been a really long day. A crappy one too. Fergie wanted to love her new job. Really, she did. But so far, it was the pits. If Fergie wanted to be a librarian, she would've been one.

Research was her jam. Well, when it was interesting. She had a knack for sniffing out information and compiling easy-to-read spreadsheets and timelines. It wasn't the hard work that annoyed her. Her complaint was the content. The actual stuff her new boss had her looking up. It was beyond boring.

Why an enormous conglomerate like L-Corp needed old land surveys, cross-referenced with newspaper reports on accidents, crimes, etcetera.

She had no idea. She'd been at it for weeks now. So far, she'd researched six locations given via GPS coordinates across Hudson County. Her new boss wanted everything, every little insignificant piece of information she could dig up.

That was the easy part. It was the hassle of the actual job that really made her want to give up. Every day she had to drive to Bayonne to pick up her work laptop she'd dropped off the night before with all of that day's findings. Every single night they wiped her computer clean.

Like she was going to run away with the secrets of what happened on 2nd and Washington sixty-years ago. Can you say paranoid? Ugh.

Fergie had always looked forward to working for a huge global company. It was supposed to be her ticket out of the Garden State. Traveling the globe, seeing new things, visiting far-off places was always a secret dream of hers. Well, that, and having her own walk-in closet full of gorgeous designer shoes.

Best secret dream evah! In her opinion, anyway. What woman didn't love shoes? Fergie hummed as she daydreamed about rows and rows of Blahnik's, Jimmy Choo's, Garavani's, Ferragamo's, and her personal favorites, Louboutin's on every shelf!

Don't judge. Fergie wasn't shallow, she just liked pretty things. Haters gonna hate. But every time she ran across a thrift or second-chance store, she'd search high and low to see what they had. That was how she'd scored the pumps on her feet.

They made her feel good about herself. Being five-foot two-inches short with more curves than a racetrack, Fergie had had more than her fair share of self-esteem issues growing up. Alright, so she was chubby. She could admit that proudly now.

If everyone looked the same, the world would be one boring as hell place. Fergie liked herself perfectly fine these days, in spite of all the times her step-monster tried to make her diet growing up. So she liked food and shoes. Big deal.

She worked hard to feed and clothe herself, so as far as she was concerned, no one had a right to comment. So what if she wanted some excitement in her life? Fergie was aware she was better off than most, but what was wrong with having goals?

She'd spent a lot of time thinking about how a woman like her could have an adventure. Travelling was the only thing she could think of. Of course, she'd been hoping this job would be the answer to that. Even travelling for work was better than being stuck.

Sigh.

So far, her plans had fallen flat, but hey, at least she was earning a paycheck. Her new boss, Mr. Offner, might be a strange man, but he signed her checks, and that was enough for now. Fergie had never seen more than a glimpse of him. All of her instructions usually came via email.

Most of the time she was able to compile her research quickly, then she'd head back to the office to organize it into neat little spreadsheets, and finally, she'd hand it all in with her laptop. But not today.

Mr. Offner sent her an email detailing everything she could dig up on one of the oldest places on record in the county. Of course, land surveys that old, along with police reports, newspaper articles, deeds, and sales records were nowhere she could easily access them.

After wasting hours at both the court house and municipal building, Fergie had been directed to the *second* public library. Apparently anything over a hundred years old was filed away in the godforsaken place. She'd been shocked to find an entire room filled with musty old archives. And wouldn't you know it, there was no cell service and no internet access. Plus, their phone lines were down. She'd had to photograph each page using her cell. When she got home later, she would send those photos like a fax to her boss along with her spreadsheet. If she could manage that before collapsing into bed.

Troy Waman looked down at his smartphone to the little red arrow blinking on his map app, indicating he had reached his destination. He frowned pensively before shaking his head.

"What a fucking shithole," he murmured to himself as he exited the nondescript black SUV his Station Master, Rex, had given him for the job.

"Try not to scratch it," the tough Bear shifter had said with a barely contained growl after their meeting the day before last. After a thousand years of waiting, The *Wardens of Terra* were being called to duty and this was Troy's first assignment.

It took him a day and a half to make his way to Shadowland, New York from the little suburb in Virginia Beach where his Station was located. There were dozens of them across the continental United States and even more overseas, though he'd rarely been out of the county himself.

Troy rolled his shoulders and exhaled. He was the first from his Station to be called to duty. A fact that left him both proud and humbled at the same time. He'd trained damn hard since he was a child waiting for such an opportunity. Now he had it, and it was almost too much to bear.

Fuck and damn. It's time Troy, get your ass in gear. That was all the sympathy he had for himself. Why the hell should he have any at all? Troy Waman was no tenderfoot normal. He was a Warden of Terra. He didn't need to remind himself of the honor and duty that went along with his position.

The *Wardens of Terra* were an ancient group of elite warriors. All of them Shifters. Identified in their youth and trained throughout their preternaturally long lives, they were guardians as well as fighters. *Station Masters* led teams of Wardens across the planet.

Though they'd been deactivated sometime in the last millennium, Wardens were born, chosen, and trained every day with the distinct knowledge that someday, they'd be called upon to defend the earth. That day was here.

Troy Waman had been trained as a Warden since before he learned how to spell the word. His heritage was a mix of Anglo and Native American. His father's blood was a mix of tribes including Algonquin, Lenape, Cherokee, and a few others. He hadn't stuck around long enough for anyone to learn the rest.

He supposed he could get a DNA test, but that might raise too many questions with the normals. Especially in this day of advanced technology in biogenetics.

Besides, it was quite common in today's world to find Native American peoples descended from multiple tribes. Troy Waman was uncommon for an entirely different reason. He was a Shifter, a special race of dual natured beings with one foot in the supernatural world and one in the human. Troy was a *Thunderbird Shifter* to be exact. Something unique even amongst Shifters.

He stretched his long, lithe body as he stepped away from the vehicle. It was already dark out despite it being fairly early in the evening. *Daylight savings my ass.* He sniffed the frigid air. The unusually high winds made the cold seem even more bitter. The street lamp stuttered on the corner, a rusty fence squeaked, and a black cat crossed the street, ducking under some parked cars. Troy's frown deepened.

It looked like the setting of a B-horror flick. All it needed was some half naked co-ed to run down the street with a masked bogeyman stalking behind her, traditional blood-coated knife in hand. *Oh yeah.* They might call it *Shadowland Nightmare* or something equally cheesy.

He stopped his musings and used his heightened senses to take in the downtrodden area around him. It would seem upstate New York wasn't all orchards and sprawling suburbs. He smirked as the "I love New York" song ran through his head. *Yeah, right.*

Apparently, parts of the Empire State were as fucked up as the street where he was born in Newark, New Jersey. He'd visited that shithole back when he was in his teens just out of curiosity. What a mistake that had been! He'd left almost as soon as he'd arrived. His extended family had been, shall we say, less than welcoming.

His gray-haired grandmother had screamed and crossed herself when he stepped over her threshold. He was what they called a *skin walker*. They feared and loathed him as something evil. Him evil? Like he was the motherfucker who knocked-up some unsuspecting normal and left her ass with a Shifter baby.

He was not evil, but he was something they did not understand. He'd been angry and ashamed that day. He'd crashed through his grandmother's kitchen to hitch a ride back down to his Station in Virginia Beach.

In his youth it was more like a military training camp, but it was all he knew of home. After all, it was where he'd lived his entire life. He'd made his peace and settled fully into his life there.

The incident with his grandmother had happened over a decade ago, when Troy had stolen his records out of Rex's office. Still, the memory remained fresh in his mind as if it were only yesterday. The fucked-up street where he was standing only brought back the painful reminder that he'd come from the same kind of squalor. *Fuck this*, he thought.

The pungent scent of despair washed over him. *Reminding him.* A young man with a hood pulled up over his head, eyed him from the street corner. *Drug dealer. Shadowland* indeed. It was an apt name for this shamble of a neighborhood.

The young man continued to stare until Troy allowed his beast to shine through. His golden eyes pinned the errant youth through the inky darkness of the night. Startled, the kid dropped the bag he was holding and ran down the alley.

Punk. Troy walked over and picked up what he had so hastily left behind. A couple of grams of crack cocaine and heroin, *probably cut with Fentanyl.* There were also various sized baggies full of what smelled like some below average marijuana and half-rotted psychedelic mushrooms.

Just your garden variety of illegal substances to be found on most street corners in neighborhoods like this one. *Fucking normals.* He frowned and dumped the still sealed contents down the closest storm drain. He sent a quick text to Rex earmarking the location.

Rex would make sure the local police department got an anonymous tip to retrieve the narcotics before someone got hurt. Recreational drug use, mainly the opioid epidemic, was wreaking havoc amongst the humans with more and more of them succumbing to their addictions.

It was troubling, but not Troy's problem. Shifters were extraordinarily hard to kill. Most human drugs had little to no effect on supernatural beings. *Normals,* he growled the thought, *such weak creatures.*

To be fair, Shifters had vices too. He just had little

experience with it. Cecil, a Station-mate of his, had an adrenaline addiction. He was always putting himself in dangerous situations, even during simple training exercises. Fernandez, a Jaguar Shifter, was always trying to get into some chick's pants. *Sex addict.* And he knew of others who channeled their energies into ways he considered to be mostly unproductive.

His opinion, for sure. He'd always been something of a loner by nature. There weren't many Thunderbird Shifters around. Hell, he was the only fucking one he knew of in this part of the world.

He didn't blame or judge his Station-mates for their proclivities. Most of the Shifters he knew had large appetites which included food, exercise, and sex.

Troy had certainly explored that part of him. He wasn't a man-whore or anything, but he'd had his share of women. None of them mattered to him. Just a means to satisfy the occasional itch.

Troy was determined to live his life as a Warden of Terra alone. He never expected to find anyone willing to share what was a potentially deadly existence.

Those who followed the Darkness and evil were always looking for ways to gain the upper hand and it was his job to stop them. The way he saw it, it was an honor and a duty to serve.

He shared this great responsibility with the entire organization. The core belief of the Wardens was based on one indisputable fact Shifters had walked the earth since the dawn of time, even before humankind; therefore, they were responsible for the well-being of the entire planet and all its inhabitants. Especially those who were inherently weaker. Mainly females and *normals*.

There were other supernaturals who believed humans, or normals as they referred to them, were a blight on the planet. Those creatures wished to destroy them and take over.

Demons, Dark Witches, and a whole plethora of evil beings sought the destruction of the normals and the world they lived in. *Idiots! Did they even realize if they destroyed the world, there would be nothing left? Where the fuck would they live?*

Of course, the supernatural world had many agencies that worked towards the common goal of saving the planet. The *Order of the Guardians,* for example, were responsible for policing the various factions of supernaturals.

Shifters generally tended to ally themselves with the Guardians. Sure, there were *bad* Shifters, but he'd never come across any willing to follow the Dark. Simply because most agreed the destruction of the world could not be allowed to happen.

Different Packs and Clans, etcetera, of course, had different ideas. Some wanted to remain secret, others wished to come out, and other still wanted to rule the weaker humans. It was a whole fucking thing, and they argued about regularly.

Troy didn't know from any of that. He spent little time in the human world. His efforts better spent making himself worthy of being a Warden. Training, exercise, and following orders. That's what Troy lived for, it was why he was chosen.

Thunderbird Shifters were very rare. *Special.* He scoffed at the stray thought. But no matter what way he looked at it, Troy was indeed unique. In more ways than one. He was born *marked* by the stars. A *Shifter of Terra.*

From infancy, he was told he carried the power of his sign within him. *Aquarius* ruled his destiny and it would aid him in the never-ending battle against the forces of darkness.

Every single Warden he knew was a Shifter like him. They were the fiercest warriors on the planet. Like many others throughout the last thousand years, Troy, *a Shifter child who was marked,* was taken from his parents and trained by his Station Master until the time when he would be called into use.

All that time, he thought, *and here I am.* He tried to ignore the pressure building inside of him. He felt anxious. His animal pressed against his psyche, comforting him with his presence.

The significance of the moment was not lost on him. The Wardens had waited a millennium to be called to act. *He* had been waiting his entire life.

"Do not fear the future, Troy," the Herald who had visited his Station said to him when he'd brought word that they had been activated, *"Your destiny awaits."*

Troy wondered if the old man referred to the Wardens finally being called to act, or if the elder spoke of yet another legend. Troy had been shocked to say the least when the Herald had entered their tidy little Station in Virginia Beach with his flowing white hair. After he told them the news, he turned to Troy and recited another old tale.

"Young Thunderbird, you are the first to return us to Terra. Do not doubt your worth. Your destiny has been written in the stars since before you were born, Troy Waman. Remember, a Warden discovers his true measure when his fated mate is thrust upon him."

Whatever the fuck that meant. Troy looked down at

his phone, then to the street sign on the corner, and finally, to the faded numbers painted on the mailbox in front of the ramble of a house his map app had brought him to.

Fuck, am I thinking? Fated mates are myths. Stories made up so orphaned Shifters would sleep through the night. He scoffed at the thought. Memories of tales the head nurse, Sr. Maria, had told him at the training camp he'd called home for years invaded his brain.

Memories were pesky things. Sometimes eternal, and always fucking portable. But he was no longer a child. *No more stories, Sister. Now, I act.*

"A thousand years we've waited, and I'm walking into a fucking scene from a bad episode of *Hoarders*," Troy shook his head and frowned at the decrepit house that sat a few hundred feet away from him.

It was cold as fuck outside and his leather jacket did little to warm him. Avian Shifters did not carry around the same bulk as other types of Shifters. He ran hotter than normals, but the single digit temperature froze him to the bone.

True, he wasn't beefy like some of his fellow Shifters, but he was just as incredibly strong, and he was wicked fast. Much stronger than any average male. He paused briefly gauging the atmosphere.

There was something off about the place. He scented *Magic* and something else. His Bird bristled beneath his skin. *Easy now.*

Lightning flashed in the darkened skies, allowing him to see the worn shingles, and cracked siding of the beaten-up colonial in greater detail. More than one window had been smashed and boarded up with cheap plywood.

If anything, it enhanced the creepy haunted house feel of the place. The porch sagged danger-ously. He wondered how the place had managed to not be condemned by the town. One thing was certain, it was an ugly little turd of a house.

Who the hell put gray siding on their house anyway? Maybe it wasn't always that color. Maybe the owner liked gray. *Whatever.* He couldn't give two shits about the siding.

His only concern was the increased supernatural activity in the area over the past two weeks. Ever since the owner, a *Mrs. Renalda Curosi,* passed away. *A haunting?*

A creaking sound floated up to his ears and he stilled his movements. The sound developed into more of a *moaning* noise. An unearthly wail. It grew louder as the lightning continued to flash in the sky.

Troy had never seen a ghost. True, there were a

lot of things in the universe he had never seen nor heard of, but that didn't make them any less real.

If ghosts were real, and they made noises, he imagined that pitiful wail was damn close to what it would sound like.

No such thing as ghosts. Yeah, well, most people had never heard of Shifters either. And yet, there he stood.

His Thunderbird shifted once more beneath his skin, the beast flexing his senses as the lightning in the air drew him to the surface. *No.* He told his other half. His human needed to be in control now. He walked across the street, keeping to the shadows.

Something was indeed off about the creepy old house. He inched further to the black door. The knocker was in the shape of a face or mask. No discernible features, just a vague impression of eyes, nose, and mouth. *Shadowland indeed.*

He listened with his enhanced hearing and frowned. There was a distinct voice somewhere beneath the moaning and creaking. A *female* voice. His curiosity was piqued.

From what he'd seen in her file, Mrs. Curosi was ninety-seven when she passed. Her closest living relative was a half-sister, a *Magdelena Kristos,* and she lived over three hours away in New Jersey. The half-sister was cut from Mrs. Curosi's will recently. She'd bequeathed her entire estate, house, bank account, and all her earthly belongings, to someone named *A. Kristos. Another sister? Maybe.*

Troy hadn't given it much thought until now. A crash sounded from inside the house. He perked up as the feminine voice he'd thought he'd heard earlier screamed in pain. *Time to act.*

Excerpt from Fangs For Nothin'

"Are you out of your mind?"

Xavier DuMont, Vampire and Prince of the Tenebris Clan out of DuMont, New Jersey, ran a hand over his face. It was almost five in the morning on Wednesday, and he was still going over the weekly requests and complaints.

He could not believe it. One after the other, he'd received dozens of requests for formal introductions for most of the eligible young females in the Clan by their parents or some family matchmaker or other. It was the 21st Century, and yet, the Vampires of the Tenebris Clan still thought he needed an arranged marriage to run things!

"No, Lucius, I assure you my mind is sound."

"How can you be thinking of going away? To some retreat? At this time of year! You know, the whole Clan is up in arms over the tax laws your father had set into motion before his demise. Some are questioning your right to rule. Then, there is still the matter of your mating—"

"Lucius, for the love of fuck! I know what is going on in my own Clan. I am even now revoking those tax laws, people will just have to be patient."

"And what about meeting with these young females? Maybe that will quell some of the unrest—"

"No! I am not inclined to take a mate at this time. My father's grave has barely begun to grow grass. There is no rush!"

"There is pressure though, sire," Lucius Redwing insisted.

He was Xavier's oldest and most reliable friend. At nearly three hundred years old, they'd known each other for a considerable length of time. Lucius had been his childhood companion when they'd fled France for the New World. After settling the town of DuMont, his father had not only been the most productive of the local normals, but he had taken over their branch of the Clan.

Breaking ties with the old regime, and establishing their own rule, the DuMonts had done exceedingly well. Of course, coming into the new century had been difficult for some, but Xavier was determined to do it, to breathe new life into the old-fashioned world of Vampires. He would see them succeed and blossom in this age that was simply exploding with technology.

"I know you have plans, sire. But the anxious mamas are already parading their daughters resumes as if they were applying for a job." Lucius grinned. He waved a manila envelope bursting with applications for audiences with him from the most prestigious Vampire families in all of DuMont.

"For fuck's sake, Luc. Get rid of them," Xavier growled, and ran a hand over his face.

"Now, now. Surely, you know enough not to disrespect tradition and courtesy. These families are your staunchest supporters. Without their aid, your ascension to leadership could be challenged. The right mate would stop all of that—"

"I will not be forced into this, Luc. If anyone wants to challenge me for the right to lead, then he or she can face me out in the open. Not hide behind some political game."

"But sire—"

"No. I will not be manipulated. You should know that of me, old friend."

"Yes. Of course." Lucius nodded, placing the hefty envelope on the corner of Xavier's desk.

Vampires did not always inherit the right to lead. Princes were not born but made. Wasn't that what his father had always said? And yet, royal blood flowed in his veins. And it was because of that blood —*his royal DuMont blood*—that so many hungry mamas yearned to tie one of their young to him for eternity.

Fortunately, Xavier had avoided them. He refused to be pressured to take any of the hungry misses for his mate, as of yet. But with his recent ascension, that pressure was now on full keel.

Shit and fuck.

"I've got an idea," Lucius said, thrusting a copy of *The Nightly News* at him.

"What is it, Luc? I am in no mood."

"Read there," his friend said, pointing at an article on the bottom left.

"A retreat? I haven't been on one of those since I was ninety."

"Yes, but remember the fun? I brought my *sheep* at the time, and you pouted because I wouldn't share her!"

"As I recall, she came quite willingly to my bed when summoned, Luc. Why do they still call them sheep? My gods, that is positively medieval!" he replied.

"In case normals see the newspaper, of course."

"Impossible. The Covens bespelled the paper to only go to supes."

"It has happened, Xavier. You know this as well as I."

"True. And Luc, I am sorry about Temple. That was your donor at the time, was it not?"

"Temple? Yes. Not to worry, sire. You always did woo the ladies without trying. Besides, now they have their own donors on hand. You do not need to bring one."

"You don't have to do that, you know."

"What?"

"Calling me sire."

"I do have to call you sire, *sire*. You are my Prince."

"Oh, do shut up. I am your friend, Luc. You've known me my entire life."

"Yes, sire."

"Luc," he growled his friend's name.

"Shall I make the arrangements then?"

"Fine. I will go to this retreat for the weekend if

only to shut you up. And to get away from all this."
He indicated the pile of correspondence.

"Very good, sire."

Excerpt from Code Wolf

"Are you fuckin' with me?"

"No, Randall, I assure you I am not fuckin' with you," Rafe Maccon eased his immense frame back into his oversized, black leather chair and narrowed his ice blue eyes at his Third and one of his oldest friends. How long had he known the man sitting in front of him?

Randall had come to Maccon City when Rafe was about ten, he looked the same then as he did now. Tall at six foot three inches, muscular, and more than a little intimidating to the Wolves under him with his long beard and equally long dark brown hair.

Rafe, however, was the Alpha. He was more amused than intimidated by his surly friend.

"A vacation?! What the fuck am I gonna do on a vacation? Come on, Rafe, this is bullshit!"

The door to Rafe's private office flew open and in strolled a very happy, very pregnant Charley Maccon, Rafe's wife. The Alpha's eyes glowed as they landed on his positively glowing mate. She wore a long, flowy dress. The shade was a pale-yellow color that, Randall admitted to himself, looked damn good with her creamy complexion and curly dark hair.

Their Alpha Female was quite something. There wasn't a Wolf Guard in the place who wouldn't lay down his/her life for her.

"Well, maybe you should consider a vacation to be a relaxing experience, Randy," she dropped a kiss on Randall's cheek and walked past him, over to her husband whom she kissed full on the mouth.

The way his Alpha's eyes homed in on her when she opened the door was nothing compared to the hungry gaze that followed her across the room.

Randall had noticed it took a while for Rafe to get used to his mate's habit of greeting everyone with a kiss or hug. Wolves were protective of their mates, but Randall thought his Alpha was doing an exceedingly good job of hiding his tension. Werewolves did not share very well.

Charley; however, had stood firm. That was the

way she was raised, and she wasn't going to change for any, how had she put it? Neanderthal brow-beating husband, regardless of how cute his ass was!

Randall had no direct knowledge if the "cute ass" statement was true or not. And he didn't want to know. He liked Charley though, had from the beginning. He was musically inclined and often took to one of the common rooms to strum his guitar or play a few keys on the piano.

About the Author

C.D. Gorri is a USA Today Bestselling author of steamy paranormal romance and urban fantasy. She is the creator of the Grazi Kelly Universe.

Join her mailing list here: https://www.cdgorri.com/newsletter

An avid reader with a profound love for books and literature, when she is not writing or taking care of her family, she can usually be found with a book or tablet in hand. C.D. lives in her home state of New Jersey where many of her characters or stories are based. Her tales are fast paced yet detailed with satisfying conclusions.

If you enjoy powerful heroines and loyal heroes who face relatable problems in supernatural settings, journey into the Grazi Kelly Universe today. You will find sassy, curvy heroines and sexy, love-driven heroes who find their HEAs between the pages. Werewolves, Bears, Dragons, Tigers, Witches, Romani, Lynxes, Foxes, Thunderbirds, Vampires, and many more Shifters and supernatural creatures dwell within her worlds. The most important thing is every mate in this universe is fated, loyal, and true lovers always get their happily ever afters.

Want to know how it all began? Enter the Grazi Kelly Universe with Wolf Moon: A Grazi Kelly Novel or pick up Charley's Christmas Wolf and dive into the Macconwood Pack Novel Series today.

For a complete list of C.D. Gorri's books visit her website here:

https://www.cdgorri.com/complete-book-list/

Thank you and happy reading!

del mare alla stella,
    C.D. Gorri

Follow C.D. Gorri here:
    http://www.cdgorri.com

https://www.facebook.com/Cdgorribooks
https://www.bookbub.com/authors/c-d-gorri
https://twitter.com/cgor22
https://instagram.com/cdgorri/
https://www.goodreads.com/cdgorri
https://www.tiktok.com/@cdgorriauthor